My *Dearest* Duke

A Regency Historical
Seductive Scoundrels, Book Sixteen
Formerly title Loved by the Lyon

COLLETTE CAMERON

Blue Rose Romance®

Sweet-to-Spicy Timeless Romance®

MY DEAREST DUKE
Seductive Scoundrels: A Regency Historical
Copyright © 2023 Collette Cameron®
Cover Art: Kim Killion

This book is a work of fiction. Names, characters, places, and incidents are the product of the author's imagination or are used fictitiously. Any resemblance to actual events, locales, or persons, living or dead, is coincidental.

Attn: Permissions Coordinator
Blue Rose Romance®
P.O. Box 167, Scappoose, OR 97056

eBook ISBN: 9781955259552
Print Book ISBN: 9781955259569

For Tito.

Thank you for seventeen incredible years full of laughter, joy, giggles, and so much dachshund love. Tito Tot, you adored your stuffy toys, fathered ten puppies, and loved your humans with fierce loyalty and faithfulness. Tito Mosquito, you can see and hear again, frolic, play, and wag your tail, pain-free. I will miss you forever—until I see you in heaven, Little Tito Man.

I also dedicate this book to every pet owner who has lost a beloved pet. We always know the time will come when we have to say goodbye to our precious fur babies, but we're never ready for the separation.

Seductive Scoundrels
A Diamond for a Duke
Only a Duke Would Dare
A December with a Duke
What Would a Duke Do?
Wooed by a Wicked Duke
Duchess of His Heart
Never Dance with a Duke
Earl of Wainthorpe
Earl of Scarborough
Wedding her Christmas Duke
The Debutante and the Duke
Earl of Keyworth
Loved by a Dangerous Duke
How to Win a Duke's Heart
When a Duke Desires a Lass

Check out Collette's Other Series
Daughters of Desire (Scandalous Ladies)
Highland Heather Romancing a Scot
The Blue Rose Regency Romances:
The Culpepper Misses
Castle Brides
The Honorable Rogues®
Heart of a Scot

London, England

Late evening, March 1816

Sitting in the finely appointed carriage, Vanessa Becket nervously bit her thumbnail—a bad habit she'd long-since eschewed. Or so she'd believed until she'd set herself on this daring—*utterly- mad-I-must-be-out-of-my-mind*—course.

Wiggling her feet to ease a bit of her tension, she surveyed the distinctive building poised at the end of Montpelier Row. Flanked on either side by ordinary structures, nothing in its exterior hinted at the wicked nature of what transpired inside.

As she gathered her courage to exit her conveyance and enter said building, several riders and a variety of vehicles passed the structure. To her heightened senses, their horses' hooves clacked inordinately loud on the rain dampened pavement.

Her heartbeat—an irregular staccato behind her ribcage—whooshed inordinately loud in her ears. A shiver skittered up her spine despite the unseasonably warm spring evening. She swallowed hard against the lump that had formed in her throat.

I can do this. I must.

For who else would if she didn't?

She had no one to defend her, to act as her champion, to demand recompense from the man who had wronged her.

Not anymore.

She was a woman alone in an unkind and often unforgiving world.

A pair of skinny cats slinked across the street, mangy ears pointed backward and raggedy tails downward. Leery and alert, they disappeared between two sturdy brick structures.

Vanessa rather knew how they felt.

Wary and watchful.

She gravitated her attention back to the structure that commandeered her interest. The front entrance swung open, admitting two approaching gentlemen attired in the first stare of fashion. At almost that precise moment, a pair of women, heads down and covered from top to toe with dark cloaks, glided toward what Vanessa had learned was the infamous establishment's ladies' side entrance.

So bloody typical and gallingly hypocritical.

Of its own accord, her upper lip curled a jot. Not quite a scornful sneer but a sign of her marked contempt, nonetheless.

Men needn't hide their vices the way women must. Males could parade their immoralities and depravities about proudly, but if a woman's indiscretions became known, she was utterly ruined.

Just as you'll be, Vanessa Euphemia Samantha Becket, if you're caught this night.

True, but her rapscallion stepbrother, Owen Elligon, was in *there*—the swine.

With my jewelry.

Just as he'd been the past fortnight.

Mayhap longer.

Vanessa had only taken to following him these past two weeks, and this was the eighth time he'd visited Fortuna—a notorious gaming and social club—in that interval. Most convenient that every time a piece of her jewelry had gone missing, he toddled into this gaming hell at the end of Montpelier Row.

Rotten bugger.

Vanessa clamped her teeth together as a wave of renewed wrath gripped her. She lowered her hand to her lap and grasped a handful of her cloak's black satin. Squeezing. *Squeezing.*

Owen had gone too deuced far this time, however.

Entering *her* house—*her* bedchamber!—and stealing her jewels right out from under her nose was bad enough. She itched to slap his face or box his ears. Or punch him straight in his bulbous nose. If she'd been a man, she'd have called him out long ago. The very first time he'd touched her inappropriately and made his vulgar suggestions.

She shivered again, earning her a concerned look from her stern-faced maid.

The sapphire brooch Owen had absconded with while she'd been out this morning was the final straw. Curse the spawn of Satan's black soul.

Foolish, foolish, naive girl, she berated herself. Believing Owen wouldn't discover her new hiding place—a faux book in the library.

It was as if he'd known precisely where to look.

That suspicion troubled her no small amount.

The brooch had been her first-and-twentieth birthday gift from Mama and was her most treasured possession. The unique piece of jewelry had been handed down from mother to eldest daughter for over a century. Each mother had shared the legend of the sapphire brooch with her daughter, too. And each woman had worn the treasured piece on their wedding day.

Vanessa allowed her eyelids to drift close as she recalled Mama's kind, lyrical voice.

"Nessa, my darling. If an unwed man shows the brooch to a single woman and she *asks* to try it on at once, she's a foolish choice for a bride. But, if she permits him to *offer* to let her try it on, then she's a wise choice, and he should marry her."

Vanessa scrunched her nose as she opened her eyes.

Shouldn't it be the other way around since the women of the family had possession of the brooch?

It made no difference.

Vanessa didn't believe in such stuff and nonsense.

Still, the brooch was a priceless family heirloom, and without a morsel of remorse, Owen had stolen her heritage. Truth be told, the dishonest cur had been stealing, first from his father and then from her family, for as long as she could recall. The blighter acted as if it was his due to help himself to whatever he wished whenever he wished.

She'd already contacted the constable and reported the other jewels stolen. Without compunction, she'd named Owen the suspected thief. The dratted, spindly investigator she'd met with had dared to chuckle at Vanessa, pooh-poohing her complaint. Treating her like an overwrought female in the midst of histrionics.

As if she'd ever resort to such theatrics.

All superfluous condescension, Mr. Wesley Dobkin had even ventured to inquire if she was positive *she* hadn't misplaced the pretty *baubles*.

Baubles worth several hundred pounds.

Nonetheless, at Vanessa's insistence, Mr. Dobkin had withdrawn a smallish, worn, black leather book from the pocket of his badly wrinkled coat, along with a stubby pencil in need of sharpening and had begun jotting down notes.

That had been three weeks ago. And not a confounded word yet as to his progress. In truth, Vanessa doubted Dobkin was even investigating Owen. Or perchance, Owen had bribed the man not to. It wasn't above her stepbrother, and she'd learned very few people turned away a generous bribe.

Right and wrong, decency and corruption, integrity and immorality, seemed melded, transient things when one might gain a coin or two.

Vanessa was reasonably confident the twig of a man assigned to her case had only been humoring her, for he claimed she had no proof that Owen was the thief.

Proof!

Who else would have trespassed so brazenly?

A servant?

Until now, she'd have sworn her well-paid staff was loyal and devoted to her.

Of course they were.

Vanessa was positive.

Well, she had been until today.

No, Owen was the culprit. Some inner instinct shouted that truth. His past behavior all but condemned him.

He'd likely sold everything of value in the townhouse he'd inherited when his father had died five years ago. In all probability, if the whispers she'd heard were true, the scapegrace had also mortgaged the place to the hilt, which was why he wanted to take up residence with her, no doubt. Not only to avoid the debt collectors but because his property might very well be sold out from under him.

Resolve engulfed Vanessa, and she notched her chin up an inch. She might be alone in the world, but she wasn't a helpless, hapless female in need of rescuing. Nor a bird-wit to be taken advantage of or exploited.

By God, she meant to see the brooch returned to her. When she once more had the jewel in her possession, she'd have Owen arrested for thievery. She mightn't have aristocratic blood running through her veins as he did, but she was acquainted with and had found favor with several titled ladies and lords.

Combined with her status as an heiress, she wasn't without influence.

Upon her arrival on Montpelier Row several minutes ago, Vanessa had discreetly pulled the royal blue velvet window covering aside—just enough to afford her an unobstructed view of the building she meant to enter this night. A deceptively benign façade that hid every manner of vice and sin.

Squinting the merest bit, she confessed to a sense of disappointment. She'd expected such a disreputable gaming hell would sport a bright ruby door at the very least—something to pronounce the place as the devil's playground.

Another man boldly strode up and rapped his cane's silver handle upon the unpretentious entry. He was promptly admitted by a giant of a man, who looked up and down the street before shutting the door.

The notorious Fortuna gaming hell and social club.

Owned and operated by the equally notorious Mrs. Jessie Dorrian-Lane—The Wicked Widow of Whitechapel.

A little shudder raised Vanessa's nape hairs.

Surely she didn't honestly wish to know how the Widow of Whitechapel had earned her unflattering title.

Mrs. Dorrian-Lane was a matchmaker extraordinaire, providing services to only the most elite clients–according to the twitchy cook's helper, whom Vanessa had bribed information from these past weeks. Or rather, her footman had bribed the girl on Vanessa's behalf.

Eyeing her dubiously from across the carriage, that same footman, Leroy Gaines, sat beside his betrothed, who was also Vanessa's lady's maid and chaperone, Daisy Struthers.

"This is the height of folly, Miss," the large, well-muscled man grumbled for at least the sixth time. Serving the family for ten years, he leaned forward a fraction as if to impart the urgency of his words. "Once you're inside, I cannot keep you safe. Should I try to enter Fortuna, I'll be tossed out on my backside. They only cater to rich nobs, gentry, and aristocrats."

He made the pronouncement with such authority and conviction that Vanessa couldn't help but wonder if he'd previously tried to gain admittance and been turned away. Or had he actually been tossed on *his* backside, as he had so eloquently put it?

Gaines was right, of course.

All manner of things might go wrong, and if she were of a more timorous nature, she'd order the coach home. But Vanessa wasn't a timid mouse. Never mind that her knees practically knocked together in apprehension, and her pulse fluttered so fast, it felt like a thousand winged insects zipped along her veins.

"Douse the carriage lights," Vanessa murmured, determinedly turning her attention back to the multi-story building. Having no wish to be identified, she'd walk from here—Gaines and Daisy trailing her at a discreet distance, of course.

Her midnight blue coach was sure to draw attention

if she were to alight directly in front of the gaming hell. In point of fact, though parked almost a full street away and under cover of darkness, someone might recognize the unique conveyance.

Vanessa really ought to have listened to Gaines and hired a hackney. But previous experience had taught her hackney drivers couldn't always be relied upon to remain and wait as directed. That first night she'd followed Owen, she and Daisy had disembarked the hackney to peek inside the club's windows. Their bounder of a driver had taken another fare and disappeared into the night, despite her promise of a generous tip if he waited for her.

Besides, what if Vanessa needed to make a swift escape? Yes, having her coach nearby was the wisest course of action.

Leroy snuffed the lamps, and at once, the inside of the vehicle grew dark. However, Vanessa experienced no fear. She'd never been afraid of the dark. Fine, she was a trifle uneasy, but not from the shadows gyrating against the buildings or flitting eerily across the lane.

Gas lamps cast luminous halos along the street,

though the farthest reaches remained dark and slightly ominous.

Her heart pulsed a frantic rhythm at her intention to brazenly enter an establishment of such ill-repute and retrieve her priceless heirloom.

Pray God, she wasn't too late.

Every female ancestor for over one hundred years had worn the brooch on her wedding day. If Vanessa couldn't retrieve it…

But wasn't that the point?

To date, she'd found every suitor, beau, and gentleman unsuitable.

She veered her attention to the jewelry store. Even now, were her jewels on display there? Her brooch, glittering blue and white beneath a glass countertop?

Or did the club dispose of contraband in another manner?

Greedy blackguards.

She'd asked Mr. Dobkin to visit the jewelry store for that very purpose after she'd provided him with detailed descriptions and even sketches of her missing gems. She very much suspected he had ignored that request, too. Had she taken it upon herself to make inquiries about the jewelry, the proprietor might've alerted Owen when next he attempted to sell his stolen bounty.

She couldn't take the risk of alerting Owen that she was on to his schemes.

He was up to something more than just helping himself to her valuables. Vanessa was convinced of it. Without a doubt, his machinations somehow involved her.

Mouth pulled into a grim line, Vanessa scarcely checked the unladylike curse balanced on the tip of her tongue. She felt nothing but contempt for those who frittered away their inheritances or for the people who owned or worked in such despicable establishments as Fortuna.

They were the dregs of humanity, preying on other's weaknesses and faults.

And those women who retained The Wicked Widow of Whitechapel to find husbands for them, through fair means or foul?

Weren't they also worthy of contempt?

Indeed. Why shouldn't they be?

According to the Fortuna servant Gaines had obtained information from, not all the grooms had been willing partners in the arranged unions.

Blackmail, extortion, and rigging the games had been used to garner their cooperation.

Vanessa shuddered.

Just *what* was she walking into?

2

The Sword and Shield Tavern

At the same time, three streets away

Kingston Barclay glowered darkly at the inch of amber liquid remaining in the crystal tumbler. Firmly encased in his white-knuckled grip—more evidence of the turmoil churning within him—the glass rested upon the battered rectangular table.

His third, or was it his fourth glass?

Since when had *he* needed whisky to bolster his courage?

Bloody, bloody hell.

Since he'd decided to seek The Wicked Widow of Whitechapel's assistance in acquiring a bride.

He was bloody insane.

No. He was out of options.

Desperate times and all that driveling rot.

He quaffed back the last swallow, closing his eyes and relishing the fiery trail of spirits sliding to his belly and creating a warm pool there.

Bollocks.

Kingston was really going to do it.

Barter his future dukedom and fortune for a wealthy wife now. The *now* being the most critical and relevant detail.

How else could he restore his familial lands to prosperity? Feed, clothe, and provide a roof over the heads of his three younger sisters and two brothers? Pay for their educations, dowries for the girls, and make provisions for the boys' futures as they deserved?

They'd already lost their parents and currently eked out a meager existence at Quail Hollow House outside Canterbury. While he'd been gallivanting around the world playing at being a soldier, they'd struggled to survive.

It was his duty and responsibility to provide for

them. And Kingston wanted to—nay, needed to—make up for his prior negligence.

But how exactly?

That worry had plagued him the months he recuperated in the hospital and the six months since, as well. Six months of searching for a solution in London. And each and every time he strove for an answer to the deuced conundrum that was his life, he came back to the most logical recourse.

Find a wealthy woman willing to pay handsomely to buy herself the title of future duchess. Confound it. Mayhap Kingston ought to have taken out adverts in the gossip rags. Promoted a blasted bidding war. He could've stood on the auction block and let them inspect him like a prized stallion.

In point of fact, a version of an auction was what he meant to put to The Wicked Widow of Whitechapel. She could handle the bidding and perhaps even encourage wagers on the outcome. He had no plans to bed his duchess, so he needn't worry the scars covering his shoulders, back, and arms would offend her tender sensibilities.

By Hades, pray God this path he'd chosen would spare his siblings' further humiliation and pain. Everything Kingston did now was for them.

He'd been arrogant and selfish, persuading his generous, loving parents to buy him a commission in the army and cajoling Gabriel Becket to do the same. Father had laughed and said it must be Kingston's Highland ancestor, Camden Kennedy's, warrior's blood that made him eager for the battlefield.

Young, foolish, and full of himself—Mother of God, he'd been a cocksure assling—Kingston had reveled in the thrill. In the excitement and adventure. Until the brutal, horrendous, gut-wrenching reality of war had stripped him of Gabriel Becket, his brother in spirit, if not brother by blood.

Jesus.

Kingston hadn't even been able to go home when his sister Madeline wrote that their parents had died mere weeks apart. The letter had taken six months to reach him. At just seventeen, she'd been left to care for their four younger siblings. And God curse Kingston for a selfish, neglectful bastard, he'd let her do so for almost three more years.

But you couldn't have known father had made several poor business decisions that rendered the family coffers empty. Nor can you be faulted that Father didn't tell you, and he left your sisters and brothers destitute.

And there was nothing Kingston could've done while convalescing either.

Nevertheless, shame infused him for being a self-centered, dishonorable cad. A better man would've promptly resigned his commission and returned home.

He flexed his shoulders, the familiar tautness stretching the flesh across his back, reminding him he'd barely survived. Reminding him what his purpose in life was now. What his obligation this night was.

Around him, the tavern's din ebbed and flowed, the sounds muted as if his head was beneath several feet of water.

Not a posh establishment like White's or Brooks', The Sword and Shield's clientele leaned more toward the merchant class. Respectable and well-to-do, but not elite or prestigious. Which, he supposed, was why several of the patrons kept sending curious glances toward his table, where no fewer than three nobles sat with him.

The lords' very demeanor, let alone their expensive, immaculately tailored clothing, declared them aristocrats. Yet none affected the haughty air or condescending attitude one often associated with nobility.

Kingston's thoughts meandered back to his siblings, even now awaiting his return home. What would've happened to them if he'd perished in Belgium? Bile burned his throat, and his gut coiled into a knot as appalling, inconceivable images paraded before his mind's eye.

As their next of kin, Gaylord, Duke of Caerleon, would've become their guardian, God save them.

Caerleon—Lion.

Lions were noble, dependable, social creatures.

The Caerleon dukes, to date, were nothing of the sort.

"You don't have to do this, Barclay," Pierce Chamberlain, Earl of Wainthorpe, murmured, his raven brows pulled together into a single harsh line. His almost black eyes penetrating and intense with emotion, he splayed a palm across his chest, his signet ring glowing in the candlelight. "Myself, Pembroke, Dandridge, Pennington, and half a dozen more of our other friends would gladly loan you the funds until you came into your title."

As the Duke of Caerleon's presumptive heir, Kingston would inherit a wealthy dukedom, several estates, and a slew of other entailed and unentailed properties. But his great-uncle despised Kingston as much as Kingston reviled the lecherous old sot.

The only thing Caerleon cared about was his reputation. A reputation that was so tarnished and tainted that a lifetime of servitude to the Church couldn't begin to bring a shine to it.

How bloody ironic was that?

Kingston would rather sell his soul to the devil before he asked Caerleon for a shilling. The duke hadn't a benevolent bone in his decrepit body or an inkling of kindness in his corrupt soul. He'd have demanded his pound of flesh from Kingston.

No, he'd have exacted his depraved, warped form

of payment from Madeline, Rebecca, and Dorena by selling their favors to his equally debauched cronies. Gareth and Paxton would've been Caerleon's perverse target. Hadn't the sodding degenerate attempted as much with Kingston when he'd been but a thirteen-year-old lad?

The same age Paxton was now.

And the duke had suffered a knife to his paunchy belly for his deviant inclinations.

Kingston had been going through a stage where he pretended to be a Highland warrior, and blades had fascinated him. He'd forever thank the divine powers that he carried a small dagger in his boot that fateful day. The day he'd nearly rendered Caerleon a eunuch. It would've been a service to the world should Kingston have succeeded.

"Surely there is another way," Crispin Rolston, Duke of Bainbridge, insisted, bringing Kingston back to the present.

Kingston shook his head.

He was out of funds.

Out of ideas.

Without hope or recourse.

Quail Hollow House needed a new roof and chimney before next winter. The larder was nearly empty, the fields unplanted, the floorboards rotted in several damp rooms, and the coffers nearly as empty as a church's during a famine or plague.

His brothers and sisters had suffered long enough.

Too deuced bloody long, in truth.

Eligible young ladies didn't want to wait years, perhaps decades, to become a duchess or take a chance that the funds they brought to the union would be long gone before they ever acquired the coveted title.

Then there was the matter of an heir.

Kingston didn't intend to produce one. Gareth would be his.

A match arranged by The Wicked Widow of Whitechapel *was* the only remedy. A marriage of convenience. A business arrangement with no expectations of a personal or intimate nature.

Unable to bear the sympathy he knew he'd see in his friends' eyes, Kingston poured another finger's worth of whisky into his glass, concentrating his entire focus on the mundane task.

It wasn't wise, imbibing so much, but he needed numbed faculties for what he was about to do.

A shout of laughter, followed by a throaty feminine giggle, hinted the evening's entertainment at The Sword and Shield was taking a turn in another, predictable direction.

He spared an acrid glance in the direction of the stairs where a couple, arms wrapped around each other's waists, ascended the risers. The man bent and placed a kiss on the woman's exposed shoulder, and she gave another throaty laugh.

At one time, Kingston had been no different than that young, randy buck. A callow, cocksure rogue, seeking his pleasures where he might while his siblings struggled to put food on the table and keep a fire in the hearth.

You didn't know that.

Nevertheless, self-loathing eviscerated him.

"Barclay?" Wainthorpe's query brought Kingston back to himself.

He slowly raised his tired gaze to meet his friend's

concerned eyes.

Yes, Wainthorpe and the others would loan him funds without hesitation and without interest too. Several had offered as much, and Kingston declined each and every one. He would accept no favors ever again, most especially from those he cared about.

The last favor he'd asked had cost his best friend his life and left Kingston maimed.

Scarred. Emotionally crippled.

A hollow, bitter shell of the man he used to be.

Oh, his clothing hid his mutilated flesh, but it was the memories that tormented him. That refused to heal.

Gabriel's agonizing screams…

No, I shan't think of it.

He couldn't, or he'd curl into a fetal position and wail like an inconsolable infant.

Future dukes didn't display such weaknesses. Didn't reveal how fragile they truly were—barely keeping a firm grip on their sanity. And only doing so because his sisters and brothers needed him.

He was all they had.

He *must* succeed.

So, Kingston lifted his glass in a salute and skewed his mouth into a self-deprecating grin.

"To finding a suitable bride," he quipped with false jollity.

All he asked was that whoever the woman was, she would have a good heart and treat his sisters and brothers with kindness and affection. Oh, and she must have an obscenely generous dowry, of course.

Which he intended to repay as soon as he inherited his ducal fortune.

He could only pray the old duke would cock up his toes and feed the fires of hell soon. And pray to God that he not squander his wealth away in the meanwhile. The fact that Kingston not only had to depend on that depraved sod for his inheritance but also that he gambled his future on it made him want to vomit.

Or maybe that was the whisky.

Still, repay his future duchess he would, for Kingston would be no lady's fancy man. No woman would ever hold any degree of control over him again. Women—as he'd learned in the most brutal betrayal— were never to be trusted. Blinding smiles, full, pouty mouths, sensual sighs, and supple bodies all hid venomous hearts.

Kingston didn't give ten curses that marriages were arranged for wealth and position every day amongst the *haut ton*. It was bad enough he was practically prostituting himself to gain an heiress.

Practically?

That *was* exactly what he was doing.

Selling himself, his pride—his dignity—for money.

But not his body.

He'd taken a vow of celibacy after the buxom beauty Odriana Janssen's duplicity in Belgium, mere days before the Battle of Waterloo. She'd been a spy, passing tidbits of seemingly inconsequential information along to her superiors. Information she gathered from her numerous lovers, including him.

Kingston would never know how she got word to her contact that night that Gabriel was delivering the missive or how she guessed it was to Colonel Pountney. Kingston hadn't revealed that particular detail—only that he was able to meet with her, at her request—for a half-hour dalliance because Gabriel was doing him a favor by delivering a letter.

Except, Kingston supposed, Odriana might easily have sent word with a servant. And perhaps she'd been told to report anything at all at that critical juncture.

I was a bloody imbecile.

His lust had cost him much. Too much.

Scrubbing a hand over his forehead, he tried unsuccessfully to erase the tormenting memory.

He had little enough self-respect left as it was.

Except in his beloved siblings' eyes, he was a hero.

A bloody, bloody hero.

The army had also declared him one.

"Unmitigated bravery and selfless sacrifice in the face of imminent death."

What a colossal load of horse shite.

Kingston was no hero.

Not by any stretch of the imagination or truth.

He should have died that night, not Gabriel Becket.

It didn't matter that he'd been severely burned trying to rescue Gabriel and the other soldiers. Yes, he'd managed to save the lives of four men by repeatedly reentering the burning building after the explosion. But he hadn't been able to save Gabriel—his dearest friend since childhood.

That irrefutable truth and his own self-loathing, would torment Kingston every day for the rest of his life.

He didn't even know how Gabriel's mother and sister had learned of his death or how they fared afterward. A memory flashed inside his mind, Vanessa's white-blonde hair billowing about her shoulders and her unusual amber-brown eyes twinkling with pleasure as she ran toward Gabriel, her arms outstretched.

Kingston had played the poltroon and hadn't called upon Vanessa and Mrs. Elligon once he'd left the hospital. Shame pummeled him equally for his cowardice and guilt.

How could he face them?

Answer their questions?

See the tears in their eyes?

Explain that it should have been him who died that day, but he'd been too eager to bed the lusty Belgian beauty?

His friends, sitting around the slightly wobbly table, exchanged dubious glances at his sardonic toast but remained silent. None lifted their glasses with him, not that Kingston blamed them.

Pain and remorse cleaved his chest, lancing his heart and conscience—a double-edged sword of guilt and self-castigation.

Would the dark emotions haunt him for the rest of his life?

Why shouldn't they?

"I must bid you farewell," he said. "I don't wish to keep Mrs. Dorrian-Lane waiting. In truth, I'm astounded she agreed to my request to meet with her to discuss the possibility of utilizing her matchmaking services."

With a hefty sigh and another wry grin for the sake of his solemn friends, he pushed away from the table. Straightening his newly acquired royal blue coat—tailored for this very occasion—he hid a grimace. It wouldn't do to arrive in his out-of-fashion togs. He must make an excellent impression for his plan to succeed.

After all, at present, *he* had nothing to offer.

Everything hinged on his future inheritance. It was rather like teetering on the edge of a cliff.

"Yes. I've heard Mrs. Dorrian-Lane generally reserves her services for the most unsuitable of ladies." Looking contemplative, Stanford Bancroft, Duke of Asherford, bussed a hand over his jaw. "Those who cannot manage a respectable match on their own."

Another bitter grin tipped up one side of Kingston's mouth. "I'd say that describes me to perfection. Wouldn't you?"

3

Still outside Fortuna

Vanessa leaned forward a few inches, honing her focus on another man approaching Fortuna, his gait slightly uneven.

Pished already?

Well, it had been half nine when she'd left home, and surely it must be near half ten by now. Owen was generally well into his cups by eight, foxed to his red-rimmed eyes by ten, and often passed out cold by midnight.

The tall man, his longish golden hair visible beneath his hat glinting in the street light, paused outside the door, his head canted as if he studied the exterior. Turning his head from side to side, he brought a gloved hand up to scratch the tip of his nose. After an extended moment, he shook his head, lifted a broad royal blue-clad shoulder as if in dismissal or resignation, and strode down the lane.

Well, at least one man in London had common sense.

What manner of men frequented the gaming hell in Whitechapel, anyway?

Men of Owen's ilk?

Drunkards. Wastrels. Womanizers.

Vanessa would wager they were spoiled, pockets-to-let nobles desperate for wives—make that the *fortunes* a wealthy wife would provide the rapscallions. Were the men snared into wedlock really as unwilling as Gaines had reported?

What kind of bacon brain wagered on the most inane things, as Gaines had informed her?

For instance, how many coins a demimonde could balance on her breasts?

How many olives could one stuff in one's mouth?

Oh, and her favorite stupidity: which lackwit could

go without sleep the longest while riding their horse backward through St. James's Park?

What of the women who frequented Fortuna?

Did they do so for a few hours of freedom?

Did they crave the excitement and thrill of indulging in decadent pleasures?

Of its own accord, Vanessa's attention roved from the ground floor to the upper levels where several windows glowed yellow-gold behind drawn draperies. According to Gaines, those chambers housed elegant boudoirs for patrons interested in pursuits other than gambling and drinking. Oh, and of course, the occasional arranged marriage for which The Wicked Widow was so famous.

Running her forefinger over the rough edge of her chewed thumbnail, Vanessa considered precisely what made a woman seek out Mrs. Dorrian-Lane to arrange a marriage. Desperate ones, she imagined—compromised and ruined ladies.

Or ones so unattractive that a husband must be purchased?

Buying and selling spouses.

In point of fact, the whole business was rather fascinating, in a terrifying, macabre sort of way.

Another shudder rippled across Vanessa's shoulders and down her arms, even raising the hair on her scalp. At nearly three-and-twenty-she'd been spared an unwanted marriage, but not for any lack of suitors. An heiress—even one long in the tooth, stout as a heifer, or horse-faced, which she wasn't—could always count on men lining up to woo her.

Vanessa had no interest in exchanging vows with any man who loved her money more than he did her. Well, the fortune she'd come into in eight days when her inheritance would be hers at last. She'd be free to do what she wished when she wished, and no man would dictate otherwise.

Bless you, Mama and Grandmama.

For her very wise and astute mother and grandmother had established a trust that not even her husband, should Vanessa ever choose to wed, could touch. Oh, she could access the funds whenever she wished, but her monies did not transfer to her husband upon their marriage.

A fact that Owen was not aware of.

Ire thrummed anew behind her breastbone.

Owen's repeated attempts to marry her off these past months while she was in mourning had been beyond the pale. Ever since her beloved brother, Gabriel, had died in Belgium, and dear Mama a mere month later. Vanessa was positive her vivacious mother had perished from a broken heart. Gabriel's death had simply been too much for her to bear.

Familiar, unchecked pain sluiced through Vanessa at the double loss so close together, leaving her utterly alone in the world except for a disreputable, self-serving knave of a stepbrother.

Had Owen truly blown through his entire inheritance in the five years since his father's death?

What about Patrick Elligon's business ventures?

Had Owen bankrupted them as she'd heard whispered before people averted their eyes and scurried away?

How could a man be so reckless and irresponsible?

Anger and frustration also pummeled Vanessa that after Mama's death, and Vanessa had opened her

Berkeley Square house and moved in, Owen had promptly taken it upon himself to monitor her every movement. Even having the impudence to suggest that as her only male relative, he was her guardian now, though she was of age.

Pompous windbag.

Why, the blackguard had even tried to ensconce himself at number fourteen, Berkeley Square, claiming an unmarried young woman shouldn't live alone.

The truth was, he probably had to sell his residence or couldn't afford his staff's wages since Mama wasn't paying the household expenses anymore. Or perhaps because, without a jot of compunction, Vanessa had taken the best servants with her.

However, the house was Vanessa's, left to her by her grandmother, and she assuredly did not want Owen's company—thank you very much. She'd endured sixteen years of his annoying presence after Mama had wed Patrick Elligon, thrusting Vanessa and Gabriel into the role of unwanted siblings to a spoiled, self-centered Owen.

An only child, four years her senior and two years

younger than Gabriel, he'd been nothing short of hateful to her and *especially* Gabriel from the moment their parents married. She'd been heartily glad when Owen was away at school. Of course, he was sent down so often for bad behavior that it was a wonder he'd even received a modicum of education.

She eyed the gambling hell where she'd followed her stepbrother these past few days, always accompanied by a nervous Daisy Struthers and disapproving Leroy Gaines as Vanessa developed, considered, and discarded one plan after another.

Truth be told, the theft of her sapphire brooch had been the catalyst that prompted tonight's bold scheme, the wisdom of which she still doubted.

Filling her lungs with a fortifying breath, she squared her shoulders and adjusted the black satin domino covering the upper half of her face. Her black elbow-length silk gloves followed. The flowing folds of her cloak hid a heavy purse. For she knew full well that a coin or two slipped into a palm proved the right incentive to be quite accommodating.

"I don't know how long I'll be, but wait for me,"

she told the servants, silently praying she could be in and out of Fortuna in short order.

Only if the sapphire and diamond brooch couldn't be located.

Which, quite frankly, was a genuine possibility. A probability, in point of fact, and her stomach sank at the admission.

Still, Owen must learn she meant what she said. Vanessa *would* pursue charges against him. If only to force him to keep his distance from her once and for all. She harbored no doubts that he'd see her committed and then attempt to finagle some sort of court directive naming him her guardian so he could make free with her fortune.

Would Owen go so far as to see her dead?

Honestly, she wasn't optimistic he *wouldn't* take such nefarious measures. He'd find himself sorely disenchanted if he thought to inherit, however. She'd bestowed generous settlements on her staff, but the remainder of her estate was bequeathed to charity.

Quite naturally, if there was a spy amongst her servants—and she very much suspected there was—

she'd need to expose the rotter and update her will, revoking his or her inheritance.

"I may be some time," she reiterated to the servants opposite her, their disapproving silence as loud as a tolling church bell. They'd been against this venture from the start, and Vanessa couldn't help but be touched by their protectiveness.

"Some time?" Daisy mumbled, her question sounding a death knell.

She made a little sound of distress, and Vanessa bit the inside of her cheek to quell the surge of trepidation her own statement had induced. Inhaling and exhaling thrice, she brought her chaotic pulse under control. "Depending on how swiftly I can locate Owen, that is."

And determine if he'd already pawned or wagered her brooch. Which meant she'd have to leave the areas designated for ladies' usage within the gambling hell. Gaines had provided her with a sketch of the floor plan obtained from the same disloyal kitchen servant.

Vanessa could only hope the etching was accurate. She hoped to see Owen from the ladies' observation gallery. Then, she'd either use the servants' stairs to make her way to the gentlemen's area or walk around the building to the kitchens and reenter Fortuna that way.

The kitchens were nearest the main gambling floor.

Vanessa caught her lower lip between her teeth.

Mayhap she ought to go straight there?

No, she might be caught before she located Owen.

If he'd already transferred ownership of her brooch, she'd demand it back, or the person who possessed it would be named as an accessory to theft.

She wrinkled her nose.

Was such a thing even possible?

Perhaps she ought to have hired a Bow Street Runner rather than rely upon the incompetent Mr. Dobkin.

Vanessa gave the maid and footman each a stern look, though the inside of the coach was so dark, she doubted either could see her face. A flush heated her cheeks when she considered how they'd likely pass the time until her return.

"Oh, Miss Vanessa. Do be careful, won't you?" Daisy all but pleaded, her voice ringing with worry and the husky hint of tears.

"Are you sure I cannot escort you to the door, at least?" Gaines asked.

"No." Vanessa shook her head. "Just follow me, and if something untoward occurs, then you may approach."

He carried a loaded pistol tucked into his waistband, so while Vanessa didn't feel safe exactly, she wasn't concerned with being attacked either.

With a determined tilt of her chin, she opened the door and hopped down. Attired entirely in black except for her undergarments, she hoped to pass as a widow and not garner unwanted male attention. Her mourning weeds made that subterfuge feasible.

She'd even piled her almost white hair beneath a black lace cap.

Glancing at the sooty night sky, Vanessa wasn't sure whether to be grateful or annoyed that no moon was visible. The streetlamps provided sufficient illumination as she made for Fortuna. Ears pricked, she listened for footfalls, even as she fingered the small gun in her cloak pocket.

In a matter of days, upon her third-and-twentieth birthday, she'd come into her full inheritance. Then, she meant to expunge her stepbrother from her life, once and for all.

"It's time for your comeuppance, Owen Elligon," she said as she knocked upon the door to the ladies' entrance.

The door swung open, and light spilled out onto the street, illuminating her.

Too late to turn back now.

Kingston reached the end of the street, having been unable to force himself to enter Fortuna for his appointment with the infamous matchmaker. His steps slowed, then stopped altogether.

Choosing to walk rather than ride Tito, his chestnut gelding, had seemed a good choice earlier. He'd needed to work off a degree of tension before his meeting at The Sword and Shield, and a brisk walk was just the thing. But now, he couldn't kick Tito's coppery sides and thunder away from Whitechapel as if the very flames of hell lapped at his heels.

He stood there for an interminable moment, head tucked to his chest and shoulders slumped, fighting an inner battle.

Flee or turn around?

He knew what he must do.

Pride and self-respect be hanged.

At last, drawing in a shuddery breath until his lungs ached from the fullness, Kingston swept a slightly tremorous hand over his face.

God, how had he come to this?

Relying upon the infamous Wicked Widow of Whitechapel to arrange a match for him?

Pointing his gaze skyward, he studied the cloud-strewn sky. A few intrepid stars managed to twinkle through the sooty haze that inevitably hovered over London.

Bloody stars.

Daring to shine cheerily amid the perpetual gloom.

Daring to stir Kingston's hope. That perhaps—just perhaps—this impossibly idiotic, imbecilic thing he was considering might turn out well in the end.

"*Merde.*"

Merde was a wholly insufficient expletive to describe the raging inferno gyrating within him.

Bloody sodding bollocks.

Sod fate and providence and destiny.

Sod Father, frittering away the family's modest fortune and Kingston having to marry a stranger for hers. Sod the war and Odriana Janssen's treachery, and sod the bloody urgent letter he'd given to Gabriel to deliver to Colonel Pountney in his stead.

Kingston squeezed his eyes shut, unable to breathe as white-hot pain slashed him in unrepentant waves. Bile burned his throat, and guilt pumped blood through a heart so badly mangled from grief and recrimination that he wondered how it could still beat.

And sod you, Gabriel, for being such a bloody loyal and unselfish friend. It saw you killed.

Jaw clamped so hard his facial muscles spasmed and the bones might shatter, Kingston spun on his heels. Lengthening his stride, he strode back to Fortuna. Every step threatened to dislodge his teeth and rendered another crack in his already fractured soul.

The whisky he'd consumed earlier seemed to have evaporated, for every thought was needle-sharp. Every movement, a jagged saber twist to his gut.

This was his penance for being a selfish bastard and

costing Gabriel his life.

He snorted loudly, startling a pair of scrawny cats creeping along the pavement. With frightened hisses, they tore off in the opposite direction.

A few minutes later, Kingston once more stood before the unassuming building. Filling his lungs with a fortifying, if not precisely refreshing breath, he stepped forward and rapped briskly upon the door before he could change his mind again.

At once, the panel swung open, and an intimidating Goliath of a man stared at him with narrowed, suspicious eyes.

"Kingston Barclay to see Mrs. Dorrian-Lane. She's expecting me," Kingston added for good measure. Though the unsmiling brute with deep creases lining his forehead probably already knew that fact.

Kingston would wager there was very little this man *didn't* know about the goings-on within the walls of Fortuna.

Suspicion etched deep furrows into the man's broad face, but he wordlessly moved aside.

Kingston stepped across the threshold, unable to

keep from sweeping his curious gaze over the opulent entry. It fairly screeched, *"Look at me. See, my magnificence meant to impress you."*

Definitely *not* an understatement of wealth.

According to the Duke of Asherford, Mrs. Jessie Dorrian-Lane served only the best food and alcohol to entice the most affluent clients into her extravagant web. Apparently, The Wicked Widow of Whitechapel's décor was intended to impress, as well. However, the effect was overdone, in Kingston's opinion.

His soldier's instincts still in play, he continued his careful scrutiny.

To his right, there appeared to be a gentlemen's cloakroom.

Boisterous male laughter filtered from the room to his left.

The gentlemen's lounge?

Searching his memory, Kingston recalled Fortuna's floor plan as detailed to him earlier by the Duke of Asherford. Yes, the lounge was to his left, and Mrs. Dorrian-Lane's private rooms were on the upper floors.

"I am Egeus," the ham-fisted, barrel-chested

servant intoned in a voice that sounded like carriage wheels on gravel. "This way, Mr. Barclay."

Egeus? From Shakespeare's *Midsummer Night's Dream*? Ludicrous.

Surely not the behemoth's real name.

He seemed more of a Doyle or a Mack or a Gunnar.

Kingston dutifully followed the man, unable to overlook the massive muscles flexing in Egeus's back, pulling his coat tight as he lumbered forward. What did the fellow do to maintain his strength?

Heft full-grown cattle? Oak trees? Grain wagons?

The sounds of the establishment rose and fell like waves cresting on the shore as they passed room after room. With each footstep, Kingston's dread increased, but he was no coward. He'd face his dismal future and bear the cost.

But what of the woman who would become his wife?

He'd be kind to his future duchess. Respectful and considerate. He'd not shame her, but neither would he escort her to *ton* functions. He wasn't capable of such hypocrisy.

"Pray God, I can abide the sight of her," he mumbled low to himself.

Egeus whipped his head around, the lower half of his face contorted in grim condemnation. His irate gaze speared Kingston, pinning him with hostile contempt. "As Mrs. Dorrian-Lane is always veiled, you'll never know—"

His eyes went wide then slashed to mere slits a blink later.

Swearing a stream of obscene oaths beneath his breath, he shoved brusquely past Kingston, never breaking his wrathful tread.

Obviously, politesse and finesse weren't requirements for a henchman's position.

"Absolutely no women in this area," Egeus clipped out, marching back along the corridor he and Kingston had just traversed.

A woman's shallow gasp echoed, and Kingston pivoted in time to see a flash of black skirts disappear into an alcove.

Not fast enough, my dear.

Egeus thundered to the alcove and jerked the

curtain aside.

"Out." A single sharp, uncompromising syllable that ricocheted like the report of a gunshot around the small enclosure.

Folding his arms, Kingston leaned a shoulder against the wall, curious why a woman would be sneaking around this part of Fortuna. Asherford had said the sexes were kept separate except for the rooms above, where carnal pleasures might be enjoyed for an exorbitant price.

Kingston was fairly certain Asherford had come by that knowledge firsthand.

Was this skittish minx a prostitute?

He scratched his nose before giving a dubious half-shake of his head.

Wearing black?

He supposed it was possible, but the light-skirts he'd been acquainted with tended to favor bright, arresting colors.

Odriana Janssen had adored tulip yellow and fuchsia pink.

That unsolicited recollection sobered him, and a

scowl puckered his forehead.

Then why did this woman hide?

Likely she was a lady with a curious nature. Or perchance, she was one of those women who enjoyed trysts with her lovers in places someone might come upon them. Some found the thrill of discovery quite erotic.

Kingston wasn't among them.

"I said *out*, Miss." Impatience tinted Egeus's command. "Or I'll call for the female escorts."

Egads. There were *female* Goliaths here, too?

No, not Goliaths. Amazons.

"Mi—ss," Egeus fairly growled, his breath hissing between his clenched teeth.

And still, the trespassing spitfire remained out of sight.

The sheer size of the escort half-blocking the alcove probably terrified her out of her mind.

Sympathy and admiration for the unknown woman seeped into Kingston. As well as his selfish need to arrive on time for his meeting with Mrs. Dorrian-Lane, which he highly suspected at this juncture was a futile wish.

Extracting his watch from his pocket, he kept his attention trained on the nook.

"I say, Egeus, should we keep Mrs. Dorrian-Lane waiting?" He pointedly glanced at his timepiece.

Bloody maggoty hell.

He was already five minutes late.

Not good. Blast it.

If this woman ruined his chances of making a match…

Bloody, *bloody* hell.

On the verge of gnashing his teeth, Kingston strode forward, trying to rein in his temper and pulsating frustration.

"Come now, love," he coaxed, using all his heretofore dormant charms. Every woman adored being addressed as *love,* from the lowliest washerwoman to the haughtiest noblewoman. "No need for shyness. I promise. Egeus's bark is much worse than his bite."

Actually, Kingston wasn't confident of that assertion at all.

Shooting a mocking glance at the intimidating man,

Kingston grinned at the baleful glower Egeus leveled him.

If looks could kill…

"I'm late for an appointment, my lady," Kingston cajoled. "And I would very much appreciate you deserting your hiding place since we all know you're cloistered there."

A muffled *dammit* filtered from the satin folds of the heavy draperies festooning the alcove.

Mayhap not a lady after all.

A hefty—quite unladylike—sigh of irritation followed, and a moment later, the other curtain twitched. A petite woman adorned entirely in black, from her gown to the simple satin domino covering the upper half of her face, to the lace cap atop her silvery-white hair…

Wait.

What?

Kingston's casual perusal shot back to her stunning hair.

It couldn't be.

Not here. Not now.

He only knew two women with hair that unusual, startling shade.

Gabriel's mother and his minx of a sister—Vanessa Becket.

Her attention traveled up Kingston, climbing up his chest, past his chin until her gaze rested on his face. She gasped again, this time slapping a gloved hand across her slack mouth.

She'd recognized him too.

Even behind her mask, her eyes grew round as twin moons.

Those captivating eyes.

Amber. Not quite brown, but not quite gold either.

The color of warm, sweet honey.

Whisky. Brandy. Caramel.

Yes, golden-brown caramel, fringed with unexpectedly dark, sooty lashes.

Kingston closed his eyes—hoping, praying he was wrong, but knowing in his gut that he wasn't.

His appointment with Mrs. Dorrian-Lane would have to wait. He couldn't abandon Vanessa in this cesspit of immorality—not after what happened to

Gabriel. He'd never forgive himself if something happened to her, too.

Why in the Lord's holy name was she in Fortuna?

An appalling thought cleaved him, cramping his lungs and squeezing his ribs in a crushing grip. For a horrifying instant, he thought the whisky might make a reappearance—all over Egeus's feet.

Had, God forbid, Vanessa become a demimonde?

A courtesan?

Some paunchy, middling-aged, depraved lord's mistress?

Kingston's stomach lurched again, and he swallowed hard. Twice.

Had she been driven to sell herself after Gabriel's death? Her stepfather had died some time ago, but what of her mother? Her stepbrother?

Was there no one to care for her?

A litany of thoughts shot around his mind, one right after the other, a cacophony of *whats* and *whys* he had no bloody answers to.

Egeus grunted, his suspicious gaze swinging between them. "You two know each other, Barclay?"

Vanessa's tawny gaze flicked to the brute and then whisked back to Kingston.

They positively glowed with…?

What?

"Kingston," she breathed, disbelief and perhaps a tinge of relief weighing her husky contralto. "Is it really you?"

How long had it been since he'd seen her?

Eight years? Ten?

Ever since that Christmas when Gabriel had invited him to call upon his family in London before Kingston joined his in Canterbury for the holiday.

She'd been a spirited young girl, just starting to show the signs of the beauty she'd become. He'd only ever looked at her as Gabriel's, oftentimes annoying, younger sister. Never as an alluring woman.

Even with the mask covering half of her face, there was no denying she was exquisite. Accented by the black satin, her pearly skin, so soft Kingston wanted to run a finger over her cheek, glowed in the corridor's candlelight.

With hair as fair as hers, one would expect her

rosebud lips to be peach or pink, but they were a deep berry red and slightly moist as if she'd just licked them. Never had a mouth held such appeal, and at this moment, those slightly parted lips caused a sharp surge of desire in Kingston's inexplicably too-tight trousers.

What kind of a bounder lusted after the sister of the friend whose death he was responsible for?

She must never, ever know that ugly truth.

The mahogany longcase clock standing regally farther down the corridor chimed the quarter-hour.

"Yes, Vanessa. It's me." He flicked the edge of her hideous black lace cap. "Find this in the bottom of your Grandmama's trunk?" he jested, quite adoring the way her face flushed.

"Stars above," she breathed, ignoring his teasing as a radiant smile arced her pretty mouth. She'd always ignored his teasing, even as a young girl.

A tendril of her perfume, verbena and jasmine, drifted to him. So sweet and innocent. Just like her.

"I cannot countenance it," she declared, placing a hand on his forearm and giving it a sound squeeze. Not a dainty press, but a hearty I-am-truly-happy-to-see-you squeeze. "It's so wonderful to see you."

Offering a nascent smile, still confounded at coming upon her here, Kingston took one of her gloved hands in his. At once, he was awestruck at the delicacy of her small bones.

"This is no place for you, Vanessa. Why are you here?"

"*That* is precisely what I would also like to know," came a slightly amused female voice.

5

Vanessa bit back a sharp cry of astonishment and slapped a hand to her breast at the woman's sudden appearance. Beneath her palm, her heart raced at three times its normal rate. Twice in the last few minutes, she'd been given such a start that she was at risk of apoplexy.

She should've known she'd become lost, even with a diagram to help her. Fortuna serving girl had conveniently forgotten several doors, stairs, and corridors. Perhaps the maid wasn't so disloyal, after all.

After sneaking from the ladies' observation gallery and making several wrong turns, Vanessa had become hopelessly discombobulated. Thank goodness, Fortuna contained a significant number of nooks and alcoves.

Quite convenient for avoiding detection.

A sense of direction had never been her strong suit. Just when she'd finally found what she hoped was the corridor to the main gambling area—where that rotter Owen did indeed lounge, her brooch proudly displayed upon the table—she'd come upon Kingston and the large, daunting man now impaling her with an impatient glare.

Only she hadn't known he was Kingston.

Not at first, in any event.

She *had* recognized him as the man who'd walked away from Fortuna earlier, and unreasonable disappointment had whirled through her that he'd returned.

And now, here he stood.

Kingston Barclay, Gabriel's dearest friend in the world, held her hand.

Across the corridor, what must be, given her black attire and air of authority, The Wicked Widow of Whitechapel stared at them. A filmy black veil shrouded her face, but Vanessa hadn't a doubt she saw everything.

Mrs. Dorrian-Lane moved her head as if glancing

about and flicked an elegant hand. "Back to your entertainment. There's nothing for you here."

It was only at that moment that Vanessa finally realized they'd drawn a small, enrapt audience, and unease whispered up her spine. Despite not having seen Kingston in many years, she took an involuntary step toward him.

His warmth and clean, manly scent beckoned her. He smelled of soap and shaving lather and a hint of spirits. Nonetheless, he made her feel safe in a way she hadn't felt in a very long while.

Head angled, Mrs. Dorrian-Lane put a finger to her chin and studied Vanessa for a lengthy, disconcerting moment. At least Vanessa presumed that was what the daunting woman was about. It was hard to tell exactly what went on beyond the veil.

Why did she wear it anyway?

Because she was scarred?

Pockmarked?

Or simply to create an air of mystery and intrigue?

Vanessa would be bound it was the latter.

"Who are you?" she asked Vanessa without

preamble.

"Vanessa Becket." Vanessa's response was just as succinct.

"The heiress?" Interest inflected Mrs. Dorrian-Lane's tone. "Well, well. This is wholly unexpected. Unexpected, indeed," she murmured, conjecture and calculation coloring the last two words.

Unease poked Vanessa again.

How, in heaven's name, did The Wicked Widow of Whitechapel know Vanessa was an heiress? It wasn't a secret, but as she'd never met the woman before, her knowledge of Vanessa's finances unnerved her.

What she wouldn't give to see the woman's face, her expressions.

One could learn a lot about a person from their expression. Perhaps that was why Mrs. Jessie Dorrian-Lane concealed her face.

"Very intriguing." Mrs. Dorrian-Lane turned toward Egeus and another equally gargantuan servant hovering nearby. "I'll show Mr. Barclay and Miss Becket to my private salon, Theseus. You discover how she managed to sneak this far from the ladies' compartments without being caught and ensure it never happens again."

"Yes, Mrs. Dorrian-Lane," the giant named Theseus responded before slipping away to do as bid.

"Because the minx is clever as hell," Kingston murmured.

Something burgeoned behind Vanessa's breastbone.

No one had ever called her clever.

"What's that, Mr. Barclay?" Mrs. Dorrian-Lane inquired with that hint of humor in her voice once more.

"Nothing of import, Mrs. Dorrian-Lane," he responded, giving Vanessa a private wink.

Her tummy promptly toppled over itself, and she was once again the adoring little girl trailing after her older brother and his handsome friend.

Kingston had always possessed striking good looks, but the virile man before her was breathtaking. In the years since she'd seen him, he'd become a man, fully grown. A splendid specimen of manhood, indeed.

Broad-shouldered, slim-waisted, and long-legged, he possessed sculpted features. His nose bore a slight hump she didn't recall.

Had it been broken?

When?

During the war?

Had he other war injuries?

That thought roused ruminations of Gabriel, and stabbing pain winged through her.

Had Kingston been there when Gabriel died?

Did he know what had happened?

She and Mama had been provided so few details.

Explosion. Perished in the line of duty. Sincerest regrets.

She had so many questions and shockingly few answers. But this wasn't the place to ask them.

"Come along." Kingston slipped Vanessa's elbow into the crook of his arm as they followed Mrs. Dorrian-Lane. "Let me do the talking, Vanessa," he whispered into her ear.

"Why?"

Before he could answer, Owen stumbled from the main gambling area accompanied by a diminutive, hunched over gentleman possessing inordinately large ears, a shock of graying reddish hair, and a lecherous glint igniting in his gaze when it lit upon Vanessa.

"Vanessa?"

Oh, bunions and blisters.

Owen's jaw dropped open, and he made a few inarticulate noises. His bloodshot, bleary-eyed gaze veered first to Kingston before gravitating to Mrs. Dorrian-Lane, then back to Vanessa. Sweat beaded his forehead where a shock of lank hair the shade of dirty wool clung to it.

"Whatever are you doing in Fortuna?" he asked, barely able to keep his reed-thin body upright. He swiped the hank of hair back onto his receding hairline, tottering sideways a couple of steps in the process.

She raised an eyebrow in silent reproach.

He attempted to stand taller. And failed miserably.

"Looking for you," she stated matter-of-factly.

"This is most inappropriate," he slurred, swaying on his feet in the manner a young tree does when buffeted by a sturdy breeze. "You shouldn't be here at all, let alone in an area designated exclusively for gentlemen. Have you no consideration for your reputation?"

"Some things are more important than one's reputation," she retorted.

Like catching a thieving liar.

He turned toward the fellow beside him. "I promise you, this is not typical behavior for my sister, my lord, and she assuredly regrets her imprudence."

"*Step*-sister." How dare the pished sot speak for her? Vanessa drew her shoulders back. "You needn't apologize on my account, Owen, because I most assuredly do not regret my *imprudence*."

She shot a hasty glance toward Mrs. Dorrian-Lane. Well, mayhap she did a jot, but she'd never concede that truth to Owen.

"Well. Well." The oily man beside him crept his lascivious regard over Vanessa, lingering overly long on her bosom. "*This* is the sister you spoke of, Elligon? You said she was a beauty, but I thought you exaggerated."

He licked his lips, then smiled, revealing uneven, dark yellow buckteeth.

A hare.

He looked precisely like an oversized hare. Vanessa half expected him to twitch his ears and rub his palms over his pointed face.

And he ogled her like she was a sweetmeat or a pastry he'd like to devour.

Vanessa edged even closer to Kingston.

"Well, she *is* a tasty little thing, isn't she?" The hare's perusal slid to Mrs. Dorrian-Lane, and a cunning glint entered his watery dung-brown eyes. "I do hope she hasn't retained your matchmaking services, Madam. Her brother has already promised her hand to me."

Usually a charming rogue, Kingston remained peculiarly silent, though his stiff form and the flexing of his forearm beneath Vanessa's palm revealed his agitation and suppressed fury.

At the hare's declaration, however, Vanessa went rigid. All the air left her lungs in a whoosh in the same instant. For the span of several heartbeats, she thought she might swoon. Spots danced before her eyes, and sounds became muffled and from far away.

After a moment, the dizziness passed, and fury sizzled along her veins.

How dare Owen make such a pledge?

Pigs would quote Greek philosophy before she'd marry that fetid little man. Even from a few feet away, the revolting aroma of garlic, sweat, and old cheese wafted to her. At least she *hoped* the pungent stench was old cheese.

"Is that so, Lord Pimbleton?" Mrs. Dorrian-Lane said, her tenor as cutting and glacial as an iceberg as she took in Vanessa again. "I'd say from Miss Becket's put-upon expression, she's not amenable to that arrangement."

"He has unequivocally no right. I'm of age." Heart pounding a thousand beats per minute, her stomach churning as if Vanessa were in a dinghy on the high seas during a hurricane, she focused on controlling her voice and temper. "*I* shall decide whom I marry. Not *you,* Owen. You are my stepbrother. Not my guardian, as I have informed you too many times to count."

She stabbed a finger in his direction for good measure.

"That is true," Kingston put in, a lazy grin tipping up the edges of his much too attractive mouth.

Now he decides to speak?

"I've known Miss Becket for nearly twenty years, as you are aware, Elligon." That rakish grin hardened into something quite deadly. "You are no more her guardian than I am."

Face contorted in undisguised rage, Owen stomped forward to stand before Vanessa.

He lifted his hands as if to grab her arms but stalled when Kingston growled, "I wouldn't, Elligon. Not if you value the use of your fingers. It's difficult to eat or wipe one's ass as a cripple."

Vanessa should be shocked, appalled, or horrified at his vulgar language.

She wasn't. Instead, she silently cheered.

Owen hesitated for two *tick-tocks* of the clock before dropping his hands to his sides and curling them into fists. He pushed his face near Vanessa. The aroma of spirits, onion-scented sweat, and tobacco assailed her. "You'll do as I say, Vanessa, or else…"

He wasn't allowed to finish his tirade.

With a snap of her fingers, Mrs. Dorrian-Lane summoned another pair of escorts from the shadows. At once, they joined Egeus. It was a wonder indeed that Vanessa had made it as far into the gentlemen's lair as she had with all the brawny men lurking about.

"Please see these *gentlemen* from the premises." Even veiled, Mrs. Dorrian-Lane's contempt was palatable. "They are no longer welcome at Fortuna."

"I say," objected Lord Pimbleton, full of imperious self-import as he puffed out his scrawny chest. "I'm a peer of the realm and a member of White's. *You* cannot ban *me*."

Vanessa felt certain Mrs. Dorrian-Lane smiled behind her veil. She'd wager half her fortune that it wasn't a benevolent, upward sweep of her mouth.

"*I* own Fortuna," Mrs. Dorrian-Lane reminded him icily. "I do what I wish. Your title has no bearing whatsoever on my decision. You are a cheat, and even so, you owe the house thousands of pounds, which I expect you intend to pay *promptly*."

That most definitely held an unspoken threat.

Mrs. Dorrian-Lane gravitated her attention to Owen. "And you, Mr. Elligon, are a sniveling mushroom, always hanging on the coat sleeves of others. I've only tolerated your presence this past fortnight because you lose profusely and so regularly that I would be a fool not to take advantage of your ineptitude. And unlike Pimbleton, you've paid your gambling debts thus far."

Vanessa had never met such a coldly calculating woman.

"See what you've done, Vanessa?" Owen sneered, hatred stamped upon his perspiring features. "A match between you and Pimbleton would've benefited everyone. You'll pay for this, you selfish, ungrateful wench. Just see if you don't. I'm not done with you yet."

"Come near her again, Elligon, and you'll have me to answer to." Kingston's lethal tone and flinty gaze would've intimidated a man far braver than her spineless stepbrother.

Owen blanched but remained arrogantly defiant. He'd never been one to exercise common sense. "Barclay, this is none of your affair."

"Ah, but I've made it my affair." Another smile cocked Kingston's strong mouth upward. "I promised Gabriel I'd look after his mother and sister."

Vanessa's regard snapped to his face, and she knitted her forehead in puzzlement.

He had?

So why had he never called or written all these months?

Did he even know Mama had died?

"Well, since my stepmother had the grace to die shortly after Gabriel did, you shan't have that burden foisted on you as I did."

Pain and outrage stalled Vanessa's breathing for a heartbeat.

How dare he, the ungrateful wretch?

He'd been a burden to them, practically since his father had been laid to rest. Always needing funds and sending his overdue bills to Mama to pay. Requiring certain foods to be prepared and harassing the servants to no end with his trivial demands.

"You were never responsible for us, you loathsome piece of human excrement," Vanessa said with as much composure as she could marshal. "Nor did you do a single thing to make our lives easier or provide for us. Both of which, I'll remind you, were done for you for years without a word of thanks or appreciation."

"When my father married your mother, everything she possessed should've rightfully become his," he seethed, leaning toward her. "But the bloody fool man was in love and permitted your mother to keep her monies and properties. Just as he did you."

Ah, so envy was what had chaffed his bum all these years.

She angled her head.

"No, the women of my family are intelligent and intrepid and have used those qualities to assure *their* possessions remain theirs." Slanting a glance to Mrs. Dorrian-Lane, she found the woman studying her with what might have been approval. "I'm sure Mrs. Dorrian-Lane can appreciate that sentiment."

"Indeed, I can," the proprietress acquiesced. "Well done, you and the females of your line."

"We'll see, Vanessa," Owen jeered, a drop of spittle at the corner of his mouth. "There *are* ways."

The asylum. Bedlam.

He'd have her declared insane and lock her away to suffer God only knew what horrors.

Vanessa shrank into Kingston, and he wrapped an arm around her waist in a protective gesture.

A feral sound vibrated in his throat as if he sensed her fear and would like to rip Owen limb from limb for causing it.

"Egeus, remove Mr. Elligon and Lord Pimbleton," Mrs. Dorrian-Lane snapped. "My patience is at an end with that rabble."

Owen pulled and twisted but was no match for the Egeus, who held his arm in a beefy fist and hauled him along. The other burly man followed close behind while the fourth guard remained near his employer.

Mrs. Dorrian-Lane turned and began moving again as if the whole thing hadn't occurred or was of so little import, she couldn't waste another moment on it. The train of her elegant gown swished softly on the floor as she glided away.

Vanessa had come to reclaim her brooch, and she wasn't leaving without it.

"Where is my diamond and sapphire brooch, Owen? You stole it from me today."

"Prove it, Vanessa," Owen taunted, teeth bared like

a rabid wolf.

"You've been sneaking into my house, stealing my jewelry, and pawning it for months."

"Christ on the cross," Kingston muttered, his tone as harsh as broken glass. "Bloody whoremonger."

Vanessa cast him a startled glance at the ferocity in his voice. He appeared as if he wanted to punch Owen into next Sunday. His hands were fisted, and sheer wrath sparked from his light blue eyes.

Owen slid his shifty gaze sideways, no doubt trying to contrive another taradiddle to cover his worthless, lying behind.

She squared her shoulders and jutted her chin up. "I've reported your thievery to the authorities and intend to press charges if you ever approach me or my home again."

Mrs. Dorrian-Lane paused and half-turned back toward them. "Please describe your brooch, Miss Becket."

Owen went pale again. A sickly shade of old dough. Quite unbecoming.

Likely, the lout knew full well if the gem was

located in the gaming hell, he was done for. Mrs. Dorrian-Lane didn't seem the sort to consort with thieves. At least not openly. She had a reputation to maintain, after all.

"It's quite old and diamond-shaped," Vanessa said, fully aware of the venom-filled gaze Owen stabbed her with. He'd always been jealous and petulant. "The perimeter and a cross-section are studded with small diamonds. Six large sapphires run vertically down the center."

"Titan, locate Miss Becket's brooch and bring it to my salon." Mrs. Dorrian-Lane motioned toward her remaining henchmen. "Oh, and do notify the constable about the stolen gem."

6

Vanessa couldn't help but shoot the woman a flabbergasted glance. Mrs. Dorrian-Lane must, indeed, want to keep on the authorities' favorable side.

Owen made a strangling noise as he clawed ineffectually at Egeus's hand, which gripped his arm as easily as if it were a fragile flower stem.

Titan gave a short, deferential nod. "At once, Mrs. Dorrian-Lane."

Then, moving surprisingly swiftly and with agility Vanessa wouldn't have expected from someone possessing such a large frame, Titan took his leave.

Egeus brusquely hauled Owen down the corridor. Her stepbrother protested and issued dire threats toward Vanessa and Kingston with each dragging step. He wasn't rash enough to do so against The Wicked Widow of Whitechapel.

Perhaps he possessed a modicum of common sense, after all.

Muttering filthy slurs the whole while, Lord Pimbleton followed of his own accord.

What horrid, vulgar, offensive creatures.

How could Owen have ever thought she'd agree to marry such a foul man?

"Mr. Barclay, you're already twenty minutes late for your appointment. Do not keep me waiting any longer, lest I change my mind about assisting you with your…"

Vanessa swore the woman slid a considering gaze toward her once more.

"Your…*situation.*" Mrs. Dorrian-Lane fell into step once more.

"What situation?" Vanessa whispered as Kingston, the chiseled angles of his face strained, towed her along after the proprietress. He was thinner than she'd remembered, hollows accenting his pronounced cheekbones and purplish half-moon arcs shadowing his eyes. But then, he had been at war, and God only knew what horrors he'd witnessed and suffered.

Or mayhap he'd been ill.

Precisely, why was he here tonight anyway?

He glanced down at her, his features grim and white lines bracketing his mouth. Something undefinable shone in his eyes, the color of a clear spring sky first thing in the morning. "She's meant to find me a wife. An heiress who will marry me, provide a substantial fortune, and, in turn, will become a duchess when I inherit the dukedom."

He hadn't said, "My duchess," and Vanessa somehow thought that detail was significant.

Nonetheless, she couldn't keep her jaw from sagging, and she pulled on his arm to slow his progress.

"Kingston!" Vanessa tugged harder. "You simply cannot do something so awful. Marry someone you don't care for purely for money? It's untenable. If you are short of funds, I come into my full fortune in eight days. I'd be happy to loan you, interest-free, of course, whatever you need for as long as you like."

She instinctively knew he'd never accept a gift of

money. His manly pride wouldn't permit it. But he'd been such a loyal friend to Gabriel; how could she not offer to help him? His circumstances must indeed be dire to resort to such extreme tactics.

Kingston touched her cheek with a bent knuckle, and her breathing stuttered once more.

What was wrong with her?

It must be the cumulative shock of the evening's events taking a toll on her. And having skipped dinner, of course. Yes. That was it. She was merely hungry.

A melancholy smile played around the edges of his mouth. A mouth Vanessa had noticed far too many times in the past few minutes. *That* she could not blame on hunger or nerves, and she positively refused to place a defintion upon whatever the cause was.

"You are so much like Gabriel. He had the same generous, unselfish heart."

"Mr. Barclay. *I am waiting*," Mrs. Dorrian-Lane's sing-song voice had a steely inflection that made Vanessa's skin pucker. The Wicked Widow had disappeared like a wraith into a room at the end of the corridor.

"She scares the spit out of me," Vanessa confessed in an urgent whisper, flapping her free hand around her face. "Especially that veil. Do you think she's scarred or deformed?"

Kingston chuckled, quite the most delicious masculine rumble Vanessa had ever heard, and her body hummed in a newfound awareness.

"Me too. I think she wears it to be mysterious," he said, also keeping his voice low. "She's a veritable dragon." He glanced around. "Should've named this place The Dragon's Lair, if you ask me," he quipped with a saucy wink.

A giggle slipped past Vanessa's lips before she abruptly cut it off.

A few minutes ago, she was at her wit's end, and now she giggled like a schoolgirl.

At the entrance, Kingston glanced down at her. "Shall we advance into her lair together? Present a united front?"

"Indeed, sir knight. I believe we must." Another giggled tickled her throat, but she squelched it.

The corners of his eyes crinkled in jollity as he

made a pretense of looking about again. "Alas, there are no swords or shields for which we might protect ourselves."

"I trust you to protect me." She batted her eyelashes and put the back of her hand to her forehead in a dramatic fashion.

"With my life, fair maiden," he said with another raffish wink. "Onward."

They entered the salon to find Mrs. Dorrian-Lane holding a glass of umber-colored spirits. One elegant arm crossed over her chest, she tapped her fingers impatiently on her other upper arm. Flicking her wrist, she silently waved them to a settee with practiced, imperial indolence.

Her insouciance manner didn't fool Vanessa.

She wouldn't be surprised if armed men weren't hiding behind the draperies; their pistols pointed at her and Kingston this very minute.

"Brandy? Sherry? Champagne?" their hostess offered, sounding the most cordial she had since coming upon Vanessa and Kingston.

Vanessa shook her head as she untied her mask.

She sighed in relief as she lifted the satin from her face. It hadn't been uncomfortable, but she didn't like the cloying sensation it created.

Kingston demurred, as well. "No, thank you."

His gaze caught Vanessa's, and for several heartbeats, time hung suspended. His compelling gaze probed hers, wonder and awe in the depths of his crystal-blue eyes. Little golden flecks glittered there, and she found herself never wanting to look away.

Mrs. Dorrian-Lane pointedly clearing her throat, brought Vanessa crashing back to the present.

"Miss Becket, you've thoroughly complicated my plans for Mr. Barclay," she said, coming directly to the point.

Why did Vanessa have the distinct impression the woman was taking her measure? *Again.*

"I have?" Vanessa blinked. How could she possibly have done? "May I ask in what way?"

She slid Kingston a sideways, bewildered glance.

He skewed an eyebrow upward a fraction in an "*I haven't a clue, either*" movement.

"Indeed," Mrs. Dorrian-Lane said matter of factly.

"I've concluded you and Mr. Barclay have a history of some sort. I don't normally arrange matches for gentlemen, and I hadn't decided whether to do so in his case as yet. I generally perform my matchmaking services exclusively for ladies. We have so little power in a man's world, you see."

What could Vanessa say to that?

Good Lord, she certainly wasn't here to hire the woman for that godawful purpose.

She found the notion revolting in the extreme.

"Let me save you some time, Mrs. Dorrian-Lane," Kingston interjected. "I thought perhaps you might sponsor an auction with me"—he patted his broad chest— "as the—ah—object to be bid upon. The highest bidder becomes my duchess when I inherit the title."

"My God, no!" Vanessa's objection rang loudly, causing Kingston and Mrs. Dorrian-Lane to whip their attention to her. A pregnant silence fell upon the room, punctuated by the gilded bronze Parisienne mantel clock's *tick-tock, tick-tock.*

She didn't care that she was intruding into a private matter.

Kingston couldn't be sold as if he were a stud stallion. *My God.* The humiliation and degradation.

"No, I say." Vanessa slapped a palm upon her knee for emphasis. "You're not a bloody horse or a bull or a…a *hog*, Kingston." Vanessa's voice rose on the last, and she turned to him, unsure even what to say to dissuade him from this preposterous proposition. "You cannot do it, Kingston. I shan't let you."

He arched a dark blond eyebrow in that commanding fashion she remembered.

Dash it to Hades.

She sounded like a fishwife or a harpy.

Swallowing, she composed herself.

"What would Gabriel say?" She touched his arm imploringly. "You know he'd never let you do such a thing. Surely you understand that I cannot either."

"I appreciate you championing me, Vanessa." The smile curving his mouth was sad and tender. His attention sank to her lips for a fraction before he brought it back up to her eyes.

Ah, so she wasn't the only one obsessed with lips tonight.

"I have no other means to care for my siblings," he confessed.

Lord, how much that must cost him to admit.

"Mother and father are dead, and unbeknownst to me, Father practically bankrupted the estate. The house and lands are well-nigh in ruins."

He closed his eyes for a blink, and agony wrenched her heart at his obvious suffering and poignant chagrin. To have to humble himself in such a debasing manner was beyond the pale.

Kingston's lashes fluttered, and he opened his gorgeous blue eyes.

Vanessa nearly cried out at the desolation in his gaze.

"There *is* no other way, Nessa." Emotion and perhaps desperation thickened his voice. "Even if I were to find gainful employment, it would take me years to earn the funds I need. My siblings—"

He swallowed hard, and she desperately wanted to ease his pain.

He'd used her nickname. And God above, she believed at that moment, she'd do anything to veer him from the fate he'd set before himself.

"Oh, Kingston." Vanessa shook her head, refusing to believe he'd been reduced to this. To groveling. To selling himself. Refusing to let him go through with this ludicrous endeavor. "There must be."

Mrs. Dorrian-Lane took a slow sip from her glass.

What was she thinking?

Did she never remove that dratted veil?

"I have what I believe is the perfect solution," she announced with such conviction that Vanessa and Kingston jerked their heads to look at her.

"You, Mr. Barclay," she pointed a finger at him, then directed it to Vanessa, "should marry Miss Becket."

"*What*?" They exploded in unison.

"Preposterous," Kingston said, shaking his head. "She's my best friend's sister. Not an unsuitable woman desperate for a husband."

Well, she might not be desperate for one, *but…*

"She, Mr. Barclay, is a woman *alone* in the world," Mrs. Dorrian-Lane said. "Trust me when I tell you, that is not a comfortable place for any woman, rich *or* poor."

That insight rather stunned Vanessa. In that way, she and The Wicked Widow of Whitechapel were similar. In truth, other than her devoted servants, Vanessa had no one.

No one to share her thoughts with.

No one to laugh with.

No one.

She'd actually been contemplating acquiring a pet to ease her persistent, aching loneliness. Her thoughts tumbling over one another, Vanessa sat straighter and bit the inside of her cheek.

She cast Kingston a glance from beneath her lashes.

What if...?

No. Kingston was right in this.

Of course, he was.

The idea Mrs. Dorrian-Lane proposed was ludicrous.

Absurd. Ridiculous. Comical, even.

But *was* it truly?

Vanessa needed a husband to protect her from Owen.

Kingston needed money to provide for his brothers

and sisters.

Vanessa tilted her chin and addressed The Wicked Widow. "Have any of your arranged matches ever been annulled?"

Kingston swiveled to look at her, his astonishment so complete, it was most endearing. "Vanessa…" he warned in a don't-say-another-word gravelly tenor.

"Very few, in truth." Mrs. Dorrian-Lane slowly nodded. "It's most challenging to acquire an annulment, as I'm sure you are aware, Miss Becket."

Vanessa tapped her chin as she squinted across the room, her vision focused on nothing in particular. Her mind whirled dizzily as she considered the possibilities, discarding useless conjectures with alacrity until she settled on a suitable scheme.

"Vanessa, you cannot possibly be considering her suggestion." Aghast, alarm crinkled the corners of Kingston's eyes.

She wasn't sure whether to be amused, affronted, or bewildered.

"Don't you want to marry me, Kingston?"

"I…" Staring at her, he raked a hand through his

golden mane. "It's not that I *don't* want to marry you, Vanessa. I don't want an arranged marriage, a union of convenience with *you*. We're friends, and I shouldn't want to ruin that."

Her heart flipped over at him calling them friends.

They weren't, of course.

Friends stayed in touch. Corresponded. Spent time together. Were there for one another to assist in the difficult times and celebrate the happy ones.

Kingston had been Gabriel's most trusted friend but never hers.

"I think we should discuss the advantages and disadvantages for each of us," Vanessa insisted. Surely she could make him see reason. "A temporary union between us would solve a dire dilemma for me, too."

"*Temporary*?" A scowl stitched Kingston's brow together, and the appalled look he gave her suggested she might've just eaten a handful of grubs. Large, slimy, wriggling grubs.

"Yes, temporary. As in short-term. Nonpermanent. Lasting for only a limited period of time then annulled." She grinned cheekily and swore Mrs. Dorrian-Lane chuckled behind that infuriating veil.

"A temporary union between you and I?" he reiterated, parroting her words as if he couldn't quite wrap his head around the idea. Or that the suggestion was so absurd that he couldn't countenance it.

Vanessa experienced a stab of disquiet.

Was the concept of wedding her the cause of his reticence or the suggestion of an annulment? It didn't matter. She'd been gifted an unexpectedly pleasant solution to a prickly situation, and by George, she meant to seize it.

She must make Kingston see the benefits and advantages of a union between them.

"I advise you to listen to what Miss Becket has to say, Mr. Barclay." Mrs. Dorrian-Lane set her drink aside and then sailed to the door. "I'll give you a few moments alone to discuss the situation. Naturally, should you decide to marry, even if the marriage is eventually annulled, I still collect my usual fee," she announced before sweeping from the room.

Of course, she would.

Did the mercenary woman ever do anything out of

the goodness of her heart?

Did she *have* a heart?

"Vanessa, Are you utterly mad?" Kingston exploded, jumping to his feet the moment the door snicked closed behind the woman.

A peculiar calm settled over Vanessa.

Yes. This was the answer she'd sought. She'd never imagined such a thing, but it was the perfect solution. She needed to wed Kingston every bit as much as he needed to marry her.

"Listen to me, Kingston. It makes absolute sense. We marry. I provide you with the funds you need to do whatever it is you need to do. And I am safe from Owen's attempts to marry me off or have me committed to an asylum."

A dangerous growl reverberated in Kingston's chest.

"He wouldn't dare commit you," he said with such menace that she shivered despite the roaring fire blazing behind the intricate screen.

She shook her head. "I believe he would. He's already threatened to do so. You heard him imply as much tonight too."

"I'll kill him," Kingston stated flatly. Emotionlessly.

That *was* another solution—and a tempting one, if Vanessa were wholly honest—but one that would see Kingston hanged and his brothers and sisters in the poor house. Except of course, she'd never let them be sent to the poor house.

She wasn't like Mrs. Jessie Dorrian-Lane, for pity's sake.

"No need for anything quite so dramatic, though I am flattered you'd champion me," she demurred with a pleased upward sweep of her mouth. "A bloodied nose should suffice for the rutting rotter."

Kingston made a sound somewhere between a cough and a choke before slipping once more into the composed, flippant flirt she knew so well.

"I wasn't aware your mother had died too, Nessa. Please accept my condolences. I'm sure these months have been most difficult for you."

Emotion clogged her throat, and looking down, she nodded and smoothed a hand over her black skirt. "They have been."

Vanessa wouldn't pretend otherwise. She had plenty to eat and a very comfortable home, but the grief and loneliness had taken their toll. Not to mention Owen's harping on about her getting married.

"I should warn you, Kingston. I'm given to cursing on occasion." She lifted what she hoped was a properly repentant gaze to his. "Typically, only when I'm distraught," she murmured.

In turn, he blinked rapidly and shook his head. "My God, you are a phenomenon. A rarity."

She wasn't sure that was a compliment.

However, Kingston was an answer to her prayers.

A husband she could trust not to attempt to wrest control of her fortune from her. She liked him well enough. After all, they'd known each other for decades, and he'd been Gabriel's closest confidant. He was practically family already.

A short marriage to him would resolve her issues and his, as well.

Why, it was a positively brilliant idea if she didn't say so herself.

Her imprudent foray into Fortuna had proved exceptionally fruitful, indeed.

Kingston hadn't said no yet, and Vanessa pressed home her advantage before he could, not quite believing her good fortune. "Once we're married, Kingston, Owen cannot bother me any longer. Then, after a few months, we'll have the marriage annulled."

"Why?" Hands on his narrow hips, Kingston gazed down at her.

She knitted her forehead. "I've just explained why."

Quite thoroughly too.

"No. That's not what I mean. Why would you make such a sacrifice? You aren't like the other women who seek The Wicked Widow of Whitechapel's' services. Desperate women. Ruined women. Women who've been passed over time and again. Women who have no other remedy."

He'd have saddled himself with such a woman to protect his brothers and sisters, and something warm and heavy and poignant made her heart swell.

Kingston Barclay was a good, good man.

"You're young, Vanessa. Beautiful. Accomplished."

He thinks I'm beautiful?

More delicious warmth wound through her. At this rate, she'd be half in love with him before the night ended.

Would that be so bad?

Assuredly it would if the marriage ended in a few months.

He chopped the air with his hand. "You don't have a tarnished reputation to hinder your prospects, and you're gently-bred. And soon, you'll be quite wealthy, too. You could have any man. Why me?"

"Why? Because I've known you almost my entire life. I trust you, Kingston, and I do not trust easily."

You haven't seen him in almost a decade, and he didn't even call after Gabriel's death, an unpleasant little voice dared to remind her.

She slammed the door on the annoying, unsolicited advice and turned the key in the lock.

"We can make this work," Vanessa assured him, aware of the pleading tone seeping into her speech.

"I shan't likely come into the duchy in the next few months," he informed her without compunction. "To be perfectly candid, it may be years after the dissolution of our marriage. And the gossip after the annulment will be horrendous. A shroud that will haunt you always. You'll not be accepted into society afterward," he warned, his tone compassionate.

"Pish posh. I've never cared about titles. You should know that." Vanessa gave a little roll of her shoulder and a flip of her hand. "As for society, my friends will understand, and those who don't aren't really my friends, are they?"

Many of the upper ten thousand had looked down their noses at her family. Their wealth had been attained through hard work and investments. They smelled of the shop, as she'd been informed at finishing school.

Better to smell of the shop than reek of arrogance, unkindness, and conceit.

And old cheese.

Sighing, his sculpted mouth drawn into a terse strip, Kingston cupped his nape. His hair shone gold in the candlelight, his eyes chips of blue ice. "Six months?

We'd only be married six months, and then we're free to file for an annulment and go our own way? You'd agree to those terms?"

Vanessa sat straighter, her heart climbing to her throat, and then leaned forward and gave a cautious nod.

Was he actually going to agree?

Saints above, please let him agree.

"Yes," she said. "Though, I'd hate for us to become distant or estranged. Mightn't we stay in touch afterward?"

He was her final link to Gabriel. The only person she had any attachment to in any manner except her devoted servants.

Was she mad for asking such a preposterous thing?

Wouldn't that have the tattlemongers' tongues flapping wildly? They'd give themselves black eyes in short order.

She nearly giggled at the image her musing conjured.

Kingston stared at her for so long, and with such all-pervading concentration, she began to squirm on the settee.

What did he seek with that inscrutable, probing gaze?

It felt as if he peered into her very soul, touching her spirit with that honest, frank, blue-eyed gaze.

"What if the annulment isn't granted, Vanessa?" he ventured softly after another several *tick-tocks* of the clock. "It's probable it wouldn't be."

"But why shouldn't it be? We'll keep separate residences." She waved a hand in his direction. "You, wherever it is that you'll live, and me at my Berkeley Square house."

Hands clasped behind his back, his mouth a flat line, Kingston shook his head. "That won't protect you from Elligon, and my siblings will expect to see my wife."

He was correct about the former, and she hadn't considered the latter.

"Must they know?"

A short bark of laughter slipped from between his lips. "How innocent you are, my dear. I assure you when we hastily wed that the gossip rags will print some unsavory, fabricated twaddle, and the other, more respectable news sheets will carry word of our nuptials. They will find out either by one means or another."

That was only too true.

"I'd prefer to do the telling. Besides, I shan't deceive my sisters and brothers." His humor evaporated as swiftly as it had appeared. "I have much to atone for already where they are concerned."

"I only thought to spare them pain at our eventual parting." Vanessa filled her lungs with air, holding it for several heartbeats before exhaling with a puff of her cheeks. "I don't suppose you have a solution?"

He smiled then, and the room lit up like someone had set a torch to a thousand candles. Blinded by the beauty of that smile, Vanessa blinked rather stupidly, convinced she looked like a startled deer she'd come upon once in Canterbury.

"I might. Let me ponder it and consider all the intricacies." He came to stand before her, and she couldn't help but once more appreciate what a virile specimen of manhood he was. His legs appeared all corded muscle as they flexed beneath his trousers. "May I see you home and then call upon you tomorrow?"

"Of course." The merest sliver of unease brushed across Vanessa's shoulders.

Was she making a colossal mistake?

What did she really know of *this* Kingston Barclay? The young, cheerful lad with a penchant for mischief and laughter she knew well. But his somber, somewhat altered version she knew not at all.

Had the war done that to him, combined with the deaths of his parents and near financial ruin? The mélange was enough to strain the comportment of even the most robust person.

Forcing her apprehensions into a fusty corner, Vanessa rose as he stepped near, so close his trousers brushed her skirts. Scandalously close, and yet, she made no move to rebuke him nor put space between them. Once more, his scent wafted past her nostrils, and she was certain she caught faint whiffs of musk, sandalwood, and pine.

"Thank you, Vanessa." Kingston took her hand in his and raised it to his lips. His gaze ensnared hers as he pressed his firm mouth to her knuckles.

An electric shock bolted to every extremity and

caused the most peculiar aching heaviness in her womb. And lower still.

"For what?" she managed, her voice a husky, breathy thread she scarcely recognized.

"For so selflessly and generously offering my family and me a chance for a happy future. For giving me hope." Genuine gratitude warmed his eyes, and yet, there was the merest hint of something unidentifiable in their liquid blue depths too.

Something private and guarded.

Well, it was far too soon to expect him to open up to her entirely, and the same was true of her.

"Vanessa?"

She peered up at Kingston, rather liking how delicate and feminine he made her feel. The merest hint of a beard stubbled his granite jaw, hinting at just how late the hour had grown. She had the oddest urge to run her fingertips over the roughness. To press her lips there, as well. With some effort, she collected her wayward thoughts.

"Yes?"

"Shall I take a knee and formally propose?" He still

held her hand, gently rubbing his thumb over the back of it.

Now she knew why animals so enjoyed being petted.

A wave of hilarity bubbled up from her middle at the absurd notion.

"You'll do nothing of the sort," she denied amid her laughter. "Ours isn't a love-match, so there's no need for that frilly nonsense. We'll have our solicitors draw up a settlement that is satisfactory to both of us. When I claim my inheritance in eight days"—a glance to the mantel clock revealed the hour twelve minutes past midnight—"that is, in seven days, we'll be wed by special license."

Even as Vanessa spoke so matter-of-factly, she felt like she was rushing headlong into the unknown.

Well, wasn't she?

"And it shan't bother you that our union shan't be a real marriage? You shan't have regrets?" Kingston prodded. "That it will be a charade? That there'll be no consummation or children?"

Vanessa felt the twin paths of heat scorching their

way up her cheeks.

"Will it bother *you*?" she shot back, not entirely positive why she was so flustered.

He released her hand and stepped away. "I hope to God not."

She opened her mouth to ask what he meant, but the door swung open, and Mrs. Dorrian-Lane sailed into the room.

Holding Vanessa's brooch in her open palm, she fairly trilled, "May I presume congratulations are in order?"

Near Canterbury

Ten days later

From beneath half-closed eyes, Kingston observed his dozing wife of just over eight and forty hours. He'd wed Vanessa Euphemia Samantha Becket the day after her third and twentieth birthday in a simple ceremony at her Berkeley Square house, witnessed by her maid, Daisy Struthers, the Earl of Wainthorpe, and the Duke of Asherford.

The latter two repeatedly and emphatically vowed he was out of his bloody mind at least a dozen times before Vanessa glided into the drawing room. Mouths gaping, his friends had exchanged astonished glances and said no more to dissuade Kingston from *throwing his life away.*

Owen Elligon had not been invited.

Nonetheless, Kingston made sure to have a letter delivered to the wretch's residence, making him aware that his stepsister was legally under Kingston's protection now. And should Elligon be imbecilic enough to venture within ten miles of Vanessa for as long as he drew breath, he'd feel the full power of Kingston's wrath.

Let the conniving bugger make of that what he would.

For the short ceremony, Vanessa had worn the diamond and sapphire brooch pinned at the throat of her ice-blue and white satin gown that Mrs. Dorrian-Lane had returned to her after commenting on the uniqueness of the jewel. Clearly, the brooch held great sentimental value, but Vanessa hadn't explained why.

Kingston had meant to inquire, but a number of tasks had distracted him from doing so.

Unfortunately, her other jewels had been sold, and their whereabouts were unknown. Kingston had fleetingly considered hiring an investigator to search for them, but reality had swiftly nixed that idea. Simply put, he didn't have excess funds to spend on such a venture, particularly when a positive outcome was as likely as Vanessa wanting to remain married to him.

Remain married?

Where had that utterly absurd thought come from?

Is it ridiculous? Really?

Unable to help himself, he looked his fill, memorizing every delicate sloping angle of her face and lush contour of her body.

Vanessa had been an ethereal vision descended straight from heaven in her finery on their wedding day. Kingston made a mental note to purchase earrings to compliment the brooch and give it to her as a belated birthday gift. Except, once she'd transferred a portion of the monies to his account, the irony struck him full force.

Buying her a gift with her coin was the height of poor taste. Besides, there were many, many things the funds could be better put to use for other than fancy baubles for his stunning new wife. She required no adornment to enhance her beauty.

Since boarding the coach yesterday morning, they'd chatted about all manner of nonsensical trivialities. However, today, Vanessa's eyelids had repeatedly drifted low until, at last, sleep had claimed her. The past few days had no doubt been exhausting for her, as well.

He'd been tempted to disembark the equipage and ride Tito. Tied to the back of the coach, the gelding had given him a gimlet eye each time the coach had stopped as if to say, "Do spare me further indignity and take your place upon my back rather than sit within the coach like an insipid dandy."

Though Kingston loved the faithful horse who'd seen him through adolescence and a bloody war, he couldn't tear himself from Vanessa's presence. She sat curled into the comfortable coach's opposite corner, pretty lips slightly parted and a pink flush on her ivory cheeks. Her eyelashes, several shades darker than her moon-spun hair, kissed her high cheekbones as she slept.

God, but she was exquisite.

From her delicate features and her porcelain skin to her bountiful bosom, tapered waist, and full, rounded hips, she was temptation personified. Such seductive shapeliness wasn't common in a woman of her slight stature.

Though he'd chosen to do penance by remaining celibate, he was still a flesh and blood man. It came as no surprise that his passion-starved body reacted predictably when present with such feminine abundance.

Kingston's gaze slowly traveled the inches from her face, peaceful in repose, to the swell of her breasts straining against her modest but expensive traveling costume. She'd opted to wear rich dark purple, the color of pansies, rather than black, and the shade did astounding things to her skin, eyes, and hair. The rest of her too.

His attention gravitated to the slow rise and fall of her chest.

Was there anything as wondrous as a woman's breasts? As she slumbered on, he permitted the rigid restraints on his imagination to relax. Were her breasts firm and round like peaches? Plump and full? Bell-shaped? Teardrops? Would they nest snuggly within his palms, or would their bounty spill over his hands?

His mouth alternately watered and went dry as a charred bone at the thought.

And what about her nipples?

Did they match her lips? Were they dusky rose, petal pink, or purple-brown?

Full and supple or small, pebbled nubs?

Kingston groaned and shifted on the velvet seat.

Lord, at this rate, he'd have a hard-as-steel erection until September.

How had Vanessa remained unmarried?

Another question he'd meant to put to her but hadn't found an opportune moment to do so as yet. For certain, she'd had offers, but one didn't simply blurt, "I'm astonished a woman your age hasn't married yet," or, "Surely you've had suitors, Vanessa. Why aren't you married?"

Behind them lumbered a second coach piled high with her luggage. It also transported five –God help him, *five*—of her most trusted servants: a housekeeper, a cook, a butler, a footman, and her lady's maid, plus a coachman and stable hand drove each of the conveyances. She'd left the rest of her staff behind to oversee the Berkeley Square house in her absence.

Since he hadn't expected any servants other than her lady's maid and a groomsman would accompany them to Quail Hollow House, he hadn't advised her that the servants' quarters had been neglected for years and were likely dilapidated. And coward that he was, he couldn't bring himself to wipe the smile from her face and tell her.

Servants accustomed to living in posh surroundings wouldn't take well to the humble quarters if they were habitable at all. In truth, he'd rarely ventured there and certainly hadn't since trotting off in his crimson and white uniform atop Tito with Gabriel at his side to slay the dragons of the civilized world.

Also unbeknownst to Vanessa, Kingston retained an agent to watch her residence for any sign of Elligon. Elligon, who had mysteriously vanished. He'd not frequented his normal haunts since Mrs. Jessie Dorrian-Lane had called for the constable.

One didn't have to wonder why.

Guilty sot.

Kingston promptly hired someone to find and tail the sod, too, although he still felt uncomfortable making free with the partial funds Vanessa had settled upon him, contract or not. However, when it came to the safety of his wife, he would spare no expense. If there was any possibility Elligon remained a risk to Vanessa, Kingston would know of it.

He roved his appreciative gaze over his wife as he'd permitted himself to do with great frequency.

My wife.

Vanessa Becket—*no, Vanessa Barclay.*

That would take some adjusting to—was, in short, an absolute delight. Intelligent, well-read, possessing a sunny disposition, and yet, the minx cursed.

Don't forget breathtakingly beautiful with that cloud of moonlit hair and those caramel eyes.

She was everything Kingston could've wanted in a wife. More than he'd ever imagined he might actually have when he'd decided to barter himself for money. *If* that was, he had wanted to take a wife—wanted to raise a family and put his dark past behind him.

Instead, he'd wed this charming, incomparable woman. A vixen he could never kiss. Never take to his bed and taste every inch of her silky soft, sweetly scented skin.

Instead, he'd call her his wife for six months.

It wasn't nearly long enough.

Kingston had instinctively known that irrefutable and gut-wrenching truth the moment they'd been declared husband and wife, and he'd placed a brotherly peck upon her forehead instead of capturing her mouth beneath his. Her verbena and jasmine perfume had snaked around him, tangling his thoughts and sending a powerful burst of desire thrumming through him.

A lifetime wouldn't be long enough with this incomparable woman, and ten minutes with her as his wife had him wondering if he mightn't bed her, after all.

Kingston knew the answer.

No. A thousand times, no.

He'd vowed never to let lust, desire, or passion rule him again.

For the thousandth time, Kingston cursed himself

for a fool for agreeing to Vanessa's scheme.

It would've been better to have wed a bucktoothed, on-the-shelf spinster or a lady with a tainted reputation than the living, breathing temptation across the coach, sleeping mere inches from him.

How in God's holy name was he to keep his hands off of her for six months? Six-and- twenty weeks? Almost one hundred and eighty-three days?

Think of Gabriel.

A groan throttled up Kingston's throat, and he pressed two fingers to the bridge of his nose, pinching it.

Vanessa's notion of separate residences was logical, especially to substantiate grounds for an annulment. Individual homes would make the situation more bearable, as well. Perhaps after introducing her to his siblings, he could consider different abodes. Especially with the entourage of servants she'd towed along.

Mayhap he would take rooms in Canterbury.

No. No.

Kingston needed—wanted—to be with his brothers

and sisters. They'd been alone and neglected far too long as it was.

Vanessa must be the one persuaded to take rooms in town. After all, she'd not even wanted his family to know they were married. She'd likely be grateful for the reprieve.

And subject her to speculation and gossip?

But what if she did so because Quail Hollow House wasn't up to par, and he, in good conscience, couldn't ask his future duchess to reside there?

A slow grin spread across his face.

It was the perfect solution.

Quail Hollow House wasn't a hovel by any means, but an heiress accustomed to the very best money could afford would undoubtedly be uncomfortable in the humble house. A house that hadn't seen any maintenance in close to a decade.

Now, truth be told, he was quite glad no improvements had been made yet. The rundown house would only substantiate the case he meant to present her.

Decision made, Kingston felt as if a great weight

had been removed. Without her about all day long and sleeping beneath the same roof, they might actually pull this temporary marriage off. Renovations were notoriously lengthy, and a six-month refurbishing was quite feasible.

Indeed, it was probable.

He'd make sure of it and thereby grant her wish for separate residences while saving himself a permanent cockstand.

Vanessa stirred and sighed before her lashes fluttered, and she opened those brandy-colored eyes. Her gaze collided with his, and a shy smile swept her petal-soft lips upward. "Did I sleep long?"

Covering a dainty yawn, she leveled upright.

"A couple of hours. We're nearly there."

She bent forward and glanced out the window. "I see the township." She cut him a sideways glance around the brim of her practical, unadorned bonnet before returning to her scrutiny of the landscape. "I've missed Canterbury."

The Becket-Elligon family had never returned to the country after Vanessa's mother had remarried.

"I thought you favored town life," he said.

At that, she flopped back into her seat and wrinkled her nose. "I suppose it's all right, but Patrick Elligon is the one who insisted we move to London. That's where most of his businesses were. However, I've always preferred the clean air and more relaxed pace of country life. I enjoy hearing roosters crowing, cows mooing, and sheep bleating."

He made a noncommittal sound, hoping she didn't become so accustomed to country life that she elected to stay on after their vows were annulled. In point of fact, he didn't know anyone who'd been divorced or had vows annulled. Both were rarities and not easily achieved.

Would it be so bad to remain married to her?

"Kingston?"

Pulling himself from his musings, he slid her a distracted glance. "*Hmm?*"

"I have a favor to ask."

Suspicion reared its ugly head. Was the vixen going to attempt to manipulate him even though the specifics of their contract said he'd repay her with interest? She'd objected to that particular, but he'd insisted it wasn't negotiable, or else the whole deal was impossible.

"What sort of favor?"

She peeped at him from beneath her lashes, then raised her gaze to meet his eyes directly. "Might I have a pet?"

"A *pet*?"

That was what she wanted?

"Yes." She fiddled with the satin ribbon of her reticule. "Owen quite disliked cats and dogs. He was cruel to them, you see. For her sake, I gave my cat Moonbeam to our prior housekeeper when we moved to London. I'd actually contemplated acquiring a dog and a cat the day we met at Fortuna."

Because the enchanting minx was lonely?

How could Kingston deny her something so trivial?

Vanessa could always take her pet with her when she left.

He gave a sharp nod and recrossed his ankles, heartily sick of sitting. "Perhaps after things have settled. I don't think now is the right time," he said, brusquer than he'd intended.

"Of course." Folding her hands neatly in her lap, she turned her profile to the window, but not before he saw a stricken expression whisk across her features. She brought her emotions under control so swiftly that he almost doubted what he'd seen.

Blast his sharp tongue.

Kingston opened his mouth to apologize, then closed it.

Perhaps it was better this way. If she became too comfortable with him, their parting would be that much more difficult.

Then why not deny her a blasted pet from the start?

Drive a wedge between them from the beginning? Because, as he'd told himself a thousand times since seeing her home from Fortuna, he was a bloody fool.

Instead of apologizing, he raised his hand and rapped a knuckle on the small door near his head.

At once, the panel slid open.

"Sir?" the coachman inquired.

"Please stop at Woolpack Inn."

"Yes, sir." The panel clicked shut.

Her head cocked, and tapping the toe of her left

foot, Vanessa examined him. "Might I inquire why we are stopping at the inn? I assumed we'd drive straight through to Quail Hollow House."

Kingston fingered the edge of his hat, sitting on the seat beside him. He scratched his nose, searching for the right words.

"That bad, is it?" she bantered.

"I beg your pardon?"

Vanessa looked pointedly at his hand. "You scratch your nose when you're discomfited or unnerved."

"I most assuredly do not."

Did he?

He lowered his hand to his lap.

Two perfectly winged brows soared high on her alabaster forehead.

He decided a tactile retreat was in order. "I think it best if I secure rooms for you at the inn. Quail Hollow only has five bedrooms, and the state of the house isn't acceptable for someone of your—*position*."

He deliberately left out mention of the deplorable condition of the long-neglected servants' quarters.

His home's leaky roof, sagging shutters, worn-out

furniture, draperies and rugs, scuffed floors, and overgrown lawns and gardens intruded upon his musings. Madeline and the others kept the house clean and tidy and tended the vegetable garden, but the irrefutable pall of poverty still hovered about the place.

"In other words, Kingston, you believe I'm too spoiled and accustomed to my comforts to stay in a home that you deem perfectly acceptable for my new brothers and sisters to live in?"

"I think no such thing. Besides, you are the one who wanted separate residences."

"Well, I changed my mind," she said on a peeved little huff.

Wait.

What had Vanessa said?

Brothers and sisters?

Botheration.

She couldn't think of them like that. Far too dangerous. Attachments might be formed that would have to be broken in September. However, rather than state the obvious and risk offending her again, Kingston chose a distraction.

"I don't recall which of my siblings you know, Vanessa." They'd been neighbors in Canterbury for years before her mother married Patrick Elligon. He scratched his nose and, at her knowing smile, immediately stopped.

He'd been an only child for almost eight years before Madeline came along, which was why he'd become so close to Gabriel. Then, his other four siblings came into the world in rapid succession, filling the house to overflowing with laughter and love.

"Madeline and I played together, if you recall. Rebecca was a trifle too young to join in our games, though she tried." She scrunched her nose, her eyes narrowed in reflection. "And your Mama had just delivered another girl before we left, but I confess I don't recall her name."

"Dorena," Kingston supplied. "She's sixteen." He shook his head. "My sisters are all young ladies now." Who'd not had any of the luxuries most gently-bred women claimed as their right. No dance lessons, finishing schools, fine gowns and slippers, assemblies, or even hair ribbons.

"And your brothers?" Vanessa asked, her interest genuine.

Kingston chuckled and uncrossed his ankles, bracing his hands on his knees. "Well, the lads, Gareth and Paxton, are every bit the precocious whelps your brother and I were."

"I should like to meet them, Kingston. I truly would. I swear I'll not swoon at the house's condition. I'm not a snob."

"I meant no offense, Vanessa. I've only been home once since leaving the hospital, and I—"

"*Hospital*?" She bolted upright. "You were in the hospital?"

Hell's bells.

He hadn't meant to reveal that. When she was around, his blasted tongue seemed to have a mind of its own.

"Why? Were you injured during a battle?" She peppered him with questions. "Are you completely recovered? Come to think of it, I did think you were a bit wan but presumed it was because of the distasteful task you'd set before yourself. Has the journey from

London been too much of a strain?"

Kingston assuredly did *not* want to explain why he'd been in the hospital.

Yet, she gazed at him, expectation and concern shining in her innocent gaze.

"I was burned after an explosion."

A deliberately set explosion. Meant to kill as many officers and soldiers as possible, but more importantly, to destroy the information Gabriel delivered to Pountney.

She fluttered her hand to the neck of her violet spencer. She fidgeted with the clasp there, face pale as milk. "Gabriel…he…he died in an explosion."

I know, my sweet. I know.

Her eyes silently asked the question Kingston hoped never to have to answer. A mixture of pain, guilt, and regret impaled him.

"I know he did, Nessa," he said sympathetically, forcing the words from his too-tight throat. Bile, bitter and hot, burned there as well, and he swallowed, hating himself—hating the sadness and grief in her stunning eyes that distress had darkened to liquid umber.

"Was it…?" She closed her eyes for one long blink, the slender column of her throat working convulsively. "Was it the same blast that killed him?" she asked in a tortured whisper.

"It was." Kingston leaned forward and took her trembling hands in his. "I tried to save him. Vanessa." Tears blurred his eyes as the memories that tormented him rose to the surface once more. "I repeatedly went into the burning building and dragged soldiers out."

"That's how you were injured," she said, clinging to his fingers. "Were you burned?"

"Yes."

Her gaze searched over him, looking for those scars.

"Mostly on my back and arms." When a timber had fallen on him.

Tears swimming in her eyes, Vanessa swallowed again. "I'm sure you would've saved him if you could have done."

Shame and guilt pummeled Kingston.

He couldn't tell her the truth.

Not now.

Not ever.

Coward. Poltroon. Weakling.

Not all the funds had been transferred to him yet, and he felt certain if she knew the unforgivable details, she'd order the coach back to London in a heartbeat and begin the process of annulling their vows.

He was a despicable, mercenary blackguard.

What I do, I do for my family, he argued.

Only your family?

Firmly disregarding the irritating voice taunting him, Kingston, instead, settled on another truth. Not the one she deserved, but it would have to do.

"There's not a day that goes by that I don't regret I couldn't trade places with him."

Her wide caramel-brown eyes rounded impossibly more enormous, and she astounded him by shaking his hands gently in hers. How had he not noticed the ring of forest green around the outside of her irises before? Or the flecks of gold shimmering in those mesmerizing depths?

"Never, *ever* say that, Kingston." Vanessa gave his hands a small shake for emphasis. "Who would care for your family? True, I've grieved terribly, but my future is secure. Without you, your sisters and brothers would've suffered greatly."

Was there ever a woman as unselfish and considerate as her? Her kindness and generosity overwhelmed Kingston. Would that he could be even fractionally worthy of her praise.

"I'm so happy you sneaked into Fortuna, Vanessa." He freed one of his hands, then lifted one of hers and brushed his lips across the back.

She wiped a droplet from the corner of her eye with a knuckle, giving him a tender smile. "And I'm glad you were there to rescue me. I cannot help but think Gabriel would have approved. Someday, will you tell me what happened? I should like to know."

8

Quail Hollow House
Thirty Minutes Later

The shy blush of dusk spread crimson, violet, and bronze hues across the horizon as the coach turned down Quail Hollow House's rutted drive. A wave of unpredictable homesickness cramped Vanessa's lungs, and she blinked back unexpected emotional tears.

So many forgotten memories scampered to the forefront of her mind: Gabriel and Kingston laughing and slapping one another on the back as they shouldered each other to get through the front door first. She and Madeline making daisy chains while plump little Rebecca tried to help.

Oh, how she'd missed Canterbury's simple quaintness.

One could draw in a lungful of air, and no pungent odors or coal dust assailed one's nostrils as it did in London. Spring was upon the land, and soon wildflowers would carpet the meadows where newborn lambs would caper and frolic. The fat buds covering the fruit trees would burst into full blossom, and songbirds' calls would fill the air.

At long last, she was home. Such peace and tranquility infused her that she believed, at that moment, marrying Kingston was the wisest thing she'd ever done. And in that same moment, a part of her wished it might be forever and not a limited-term arrangement.

They got on well, and she liked him.

More than liked him if she were completely candid.

She slid him a sideways glance, his handsome profile indecipherable. He wore the same tobacco brown coat she'd seen him wear several times before. Where once it might've hugged his wide shoulders like a second skin, there was room to spare.

Now she knew why.

The muscles flexing in his thighs proved he was still virile and strong, however.

They'd agreed his siblings wouldn't know their marriage was a business arrangement that would end in six months. Regret and something undefinable pitted in her stomach at the deception. But truth be told, she concurred with Kingston that his family should be spared further angst.

And as theirs would be an amicable dissolution of marriage, Vanessa prayed the residual damage would be minimal. In the meanwhile, she intended to do all within her power to utilize her wealth to ensure the Barclays would never want for anything again.

Allowing a private, satisfied upward bend of her mouth, she transferred her attention to the stately house less than half a mile away—her former home.

Helmstead Gate's tall, regal Tudor-style chimneys rose high above the landscape, vigilant sentinels keeping watch over the mansion and lands. Only a loyal, skeletal staff saw to the grand manor's upkeep, over three times Quail Hollow House's size.

To her knowledge, Gabriel had only visited

Helmstead Gate infrequently since purchasing his commission in the army. Yet, based on the reports provided to her each month, the place was kept in tip-top shape by the well-paid servants.

Vanessa hadn't been able to bring herself to sell the estate or reside there after inheriting it when Gabriel died. How could she? The manor and grounds had been his heritage, and they were her last connection to their father, as well.

Selling Helmstead was as inconceivable as selling her precious brooch.

She'd promptly terminated Mr. Dobkin's services after Mrs. Dorrian-Lane had returned the gem to her. The investigator had the audacity to demand Vanessa pay him for the rest of the month. To which she'd replied, he could return the funds she'd already paid him since he had made absolutely no progress in finding the jewel himself.

Her focus gravitated to Quail Hollow, and her previous sense of satisfaction faltered.

Perhaps if Quail Hollow was truly as decrepit as Kingston alluded, the entire family might remove themselves to Helmstead. Now, there was an idea that held true merit. At least until the refurbishing was complete. She would wait to assess Quail Hollow House before making any such suggestion, however.

Vanessa pressed a hand to her tummy as Kingston handed her down from the coach. Honestly, she was quite apprehensive about meeting her new brothers and sisters. Despite his insistence at Fortuna that she meet them, he'd changed his mind for some reason.

It had taken a great deal of persuading to convince him to introduce her as his new wife before shuttling her off to the inn for the duration of her stay.

Which, of course, she had absolutely no intention of doing.

However, could she oversee the improvements? Refurbishing? New wardrobes for his family? No, she needed to be nearer than Canterbury, three miles away.

He seemed to be unaware that Helmstead Gate had passed to her. There was much they didn't know about one another. Vanessa stifled the sigh building behind her breastbone.

By accompanying Kingston to Canterbury, she

could spend her funds on improvements, furnishings, linens, and so on, leaving him free to do whatever he deemed most important with the monies she'd advanced him.

With her faithful servants in tow, Vanessa was positive the house could be made inhabitable in short order. If that proved impossible, well, stately, *vacant* Helmstead Gate awaited. On the morrow, she'd send a discreet missive by way of Leroy and inform the staff to prepare the house.

Just in case things went awry here.

The shortage of bedchambers at Quail Hollow was an issue, but perhaps other rooms might be converted into temporary chambers. She searched the archives of her memory, trying to recall the house's floor plan.

At best, her recollection was fuzzy. An absence of many years contributed to the uncertainty. Besides, she'd only ever been in Madeline's bedchamber on the upper floor and the drawing room, dining room, and kitchens on the lower.

According to Kingston, Paxton and Gareth already shared a room. If she could convince two of the sisters to do so as well, then there would be sufficient bedchambers until a new wing could be built. She meant to see the addition accomplished before the annulment commenced.

Soon, the grounds would be bustling with all manner of craftsmen as well as wagons delivering supplies.

"Welcome to Quail Hollow House, Vanessa," Kingston said gravely, a note of pride in his voice despite the house's raggedy appearance. He didn't apologize for the dilapidated condition, and her heart turned over with approval and compassion.

"I have so many wonderful memories of time spent here as a child," Vanessa said, deciding truth was the best response.

The place looked tired and worn, but the bones of the building were sturdy, and the clean windows sparkled cheerily despite the disrepair. Several shutters hung askew, and vines snaked up the front of the house.

The structure looked sound enough except for a few missing chimney bricks. The setting sun cast burnished and golden hues over the aged stones, giving it a quaint, romantic ambiance.

How well she recollected the tidy gardens and the studiously cared for lawns that once graced the expansive grounds. She'd romped there often enough with Madeline, and the two of them had tagged after their adored older brothers, who spent a great deal of time in what now appeared to be empty stables.

As she visually inspected the house, two gray-brown mice scurried from beneath a pile of wood stacked haphazardly near the front entrance.

Kingston stiffened, and his breathing hitched, revealing he'd spied the tiny trespassers too.

How far the Barclays' circumstances had fallen, but Vanessa knew better than to reveal pity or empathy.

Kingston's bruised pride couldn't take another blow.

Once more, Vanessa's attention drifted toward Helmstead. Residing there might be advisable during the renovation at Quail Hollow, truth be told.

She and Kingston had taken but three steps before the black, paint-chipped entrance door flew open, and a parade of his exuberant, laughing siblings burst forth.

"Kingston," a lanky lad exclaimed, rushing forward, followed by a more somber teenager and his three grinning sisters.

Kingston dropped his hand from Vanessa's elbow as his family surrounded him, hugging, kissing, laughing, and bombarding him with questions.

After a few moments, Madeline centered her focus on Vanessa. Her eyes went round, and a smile wreathed her face. "Vanessa Becket?"

Astonishment pitched her voice high on the last syllable.

That drew her siblings' avid attention.

She slung her brother a puzzled glance before returning her attention to Vanessa, her blue eyes brimming with questions. "What in the world?"

Now, all five of his brothers and sisters openly gaped at Vanessa. She felt somewhat like an oddity on display at a country fair. Nonetheless, she summoned a genuine smile.

The family resemblance was unmistakable. All possessed blond hair and blue eyes, though Gareth's and Dorena's hair was almost light brown, while Madeline's was the shade of ripe wheat. Her eyes were also a darker blue, as were Paxton's.

Five pairs of eyes fixed on Vanessa, keen curiosity skating across their too-lean features as they considered her.

Kingston cleared his throat and tipped up one side of his mouth. "Madeline, I see you remember Vanessa."

"I do too," Rebecca piped in, a flush turning her cheeks rosy. "Though, I confess not well."

"Well, I don't," grumbled Dorena, planting her hands on her hips and looking between Vanessa and Kingston, suspicion narrowing her cornflower-blue gaze.

A slight breeze teased the worn hem of her outdated gown and ruffled her brothers' too-long hair. Wearing trousers several inches too short, the boys shifted their scuffed-boot-shod feet, casting their attention to the ground as their ears turned raspberry red.

Fine lines bracketing his mouth, Kingston reclaimed her elbow. "I'd like to introduce you to my wife."

9

"Wife?" his five siblings chorused in comical, flabbergasted unison as if they'd practiced doing so.

"*Wife?*" Dorena repeated, making the word sound like a foul oath. "You never said a word about a *wife* when you went to London, Kingston. Only that you would find a solution to our…" she exchanged guarded, private glances with her brothers and sisters. "Our circumstances."

Did they sincerely believe Vanessa wasn't aware of their impoverishment?

Well, perhaps pride was all they had left.

Fifteen-year-old Gareth scratched his chin, eyeing Vanessa from head to toe, and she regretted wearing her stylish traveling ensemble. It bespoke wealth they might misinterpret for superiority.

"Seems to me, Rena, she *is* the solution," he said with youthful candor.

The boys should be at university, getting an education, and the girls at finishing school, if they desired. Vanessa's heart ached for all they'd been deprived of.

"Kingston, you married an *heiress?*" Dorena spat the word before she gave a contemptuous snort. "*That was* your solution?"

Oh, bugger.

"Dorena." Rebecca glared darkly at her sister. "Where are your manners?"

"Indeed, Dorena," Madeline reprimanded, her tone soft but uncompromising. "You're behaving unspeakably rude to our new sis—" At the horrified glances swung to her by every other sibling, she pressed her mouth into a thin ribbon. "To Vanessa," she amended with an apologetic glance at Vanessa.

Vanessa hadn't considered she'd be an outsider. An unwelcome intruder in their tightknit family. A pang of disappointment pealed through her. Once Kingston had made it plain he'd not hide her from his family, she'd hoped to renew her friendship with Madeline and forge new ones with the other Barclays, as well.

Except…he *had* tried to foist her off at the inn.

She slanted him a considering glance from beneath her lashes.

Had he changed his mind?

Why?

"See here," Kingston said, his reproving attention settling on each of his sisters and brothers in turn. "Vanessa deserves our gratitude for consenting to join our family."

Gratitude?

Mouths pinched, mutiny glinted in Dorena and Gareth's eyes. Madeline and Rebecca darted chagrined gazes between Vanessa, Kingston, and their angry siblings. A half-grin quirking his mouth, Paxton looked on, equally amused and curious.

And there went Kingston's hand, lifted to scratch his nose.

Vanessa would be bound that he hadn't expected

her to receive a less than cordial welcome, either. His sole motivation was to make a better life for them, and he'd sacrificed himself to do so. They'd never know what depths he'd been willing to go to, what humiliation he'd have endured securing their futures, and righteous anger simmered low in her belly for him.

What would they have done had he brought home the woman who'd won him at the auction that had never taken place? God only knew what manner of person she would've been.

A most inappropriate giggle bubbled up the back of Vanessa's throat.

"I told you I'd do what needed to be done," Kingston said stiffly, sending Vanessa an apologetic glance over the blond heads surrounding him.

"You should have consulted us first," Dorena insisted heatedly.

"Aye, we should've had a say, too," Paxton ventured, but without nearly the same vehemence as his sister. "Your wife is very pretty, though, Kingston."

Dorena mouthed, "Traitor."

Paxton just shrugged his thin shoulders.

"I do not need your permission to marry," Kingston clipped out.

The six siblings all began speaking at once, and in the cacophony, several things became clear.

Not all his family welcomed Vanessa.

The Barclays—one and all—possessed an abundance of pride and loathed the idea of their brother marrying for money. Vanessa was an interloper, even if she'd been neighbors with the Barclays at one time, and Gabriel had been Kingston's closest chum. And lastly, Kingston might be their older brother and guardian, but Madeline was the one they looked to for leadership.

Vanessa couldn't get a word in edgewise, and so she patiently waited for the din to subside. The arrival of the heavily-laden second coach saw to that.

The younger Barclays' eyes grew enormous once more when the other conveyance, piled high with luggage, lumbered to a rocky stop, and five servants descended from the equipage. Her staff stretched and, with identical skeptical expressions, examined their temporary home.

Only they weren't aware it was temporary.

No one was except two solemn-faced, bespectacled solicitors whose profession required them to keep the knowledge to themselves.

However, in less time than it took for Vanessa to note that unfortunate fact, her staff had composed their features into neutral expressions as any loyal servants worth their salt did.

"Where in the Hades do you suppose we'll put *them*?" Gareth asked the disgust and apprehension he tried to hide causing his adolescent voice to crack.

"Gareth," Madeline chided. "Language."

Though she hid it well, she too fretted. Her gaze skittering between the servants patiently standing and awaiting orders and the house, gave her away. As did her tightly clasped hands.

Snorting, Gareth shook his head and kicked at a small stone.

"There are *nine* of them," he grumbled. "And the servants' quarters are meant for four. And need I remind you, Madeline, they've been unused for years? Cobwebs. Rodents. Peeling paper. Rotting floors? Leaky roof?"

Vanessa caught the horrified expression that whisked across Daisy's face before the lady's maid schooled her features into a mask of indifference. But not before she sent Leroy Gaines an I-told-you-so-look.

"That is true," Rebecca put in, worry etching the corners of her pretty but thin face.

Room for four?

Truly?

Why hadn't Kingston said anything?

Because—the truth rammed her with the force of a coal cart— he hadn't intended for her or her servants to actually stay at Quail Hollow.

What had changed his mind?

He'd been insistent that she meet his family when they were in London.

This was most awkward.

A chagrined flush crept up Vanessa's throat and heated her face to her hairline. She looked at her new husband, trying to keep the accusation from her gaze.

"I'm certain we can make temporary arrangements," she said. "We may be a bit crowded, but only for a day or two until something can be worked out."

Helmstead sounded more and more appealing with each passing minute.

"Yes, of course we can." Madeline gave her sisters a *don't-you-dare-argue* look. "I'll move my things in with Rebecca, and Kingston and Vanessa can sleep in Mama and Papa's chamber. The female servants can use Dorena's chamber—"

"What?" Dorena huffed, blue sparks spewing from her eyes. "I have to share a chamber with you *and* Rebecca?"

"We are *all* making sacrifices, Dorena," Madeline warned in a no-nonsense tone.

That left one bedchamber.

Vanessa opened her mouth to say she and Kingston wouldn't be sharing a bedchamber, but before she could, Madeline said, "The male house servants can take the last room inside the house. There are lodgings in the stables for the drivers and stable hands, but I fear they're in poor repair, as well."

To their credit, Vanessa's servants remained bland-faced.

"That sounds perfectly acceptable for tonight," she said, refusing to send her staff an apologetic glance. It would also do them good to appreciate how well off they had it.

Kingston nodded his agreement. "We'll make do for tonight, and tomorrow, I'll determine what needs to be done first to make everyone comfortable."

No doubt, he thought to bundle her and her servants back to Canterbury.

In short order, everyone had been shown to their rooms, and the servants were busily preparing the evening meal, unpacking, or attending to the horseflesh.

Vanessa stood in the center of the chamber she would share with Kingston. She'd removed her outerwear and instructed Daisy to wait to unpack her trunks before sending her below to assist with supper.

Thank God, Vanessa had the forethought to bring foodstuffs. For from what Daisy had relayed to her, there wasn't enough in the larder to feed two people, let alone sixteen. No wonder the Barclay brood looked half-starved.

Kingston was indeed in dire financial straits.

She eyed the tidy bed placed beneath a window, matching bed tables on either side. It was the same size as her Berkeley Square bed, yet when she contemplated sharing it with Kingston, the thing seemed much, *much* too small.

Or was it, at two inches over six feet, he was much, much too large compared to her five-foot-three stature?

But how could she selfishly demand her own room when everyone was sleeping two or three in a bedchamber?

She couldn't, of course.

How can you hope to convince anyone your marriage has not been consummated if you're sharing a room with your husband?

A single, soft knock echoed at the door.

"Come in," she called, hoping it was anyone other than her Kingston. She wasn't quite ready to face him yet. To suggest they move everyone to Helmstead Gate, post haste.

He poked his head inside, a grin teasing one side of his mouth and a shock of blond hair falling boyishly over his brow. His eyes, however, held a gravity that made her nervous. "May I come in?"

Bollocks.

"It's your chamber too." Filling her lungs with fortifying air, she waved her hand.

He advanced inside and closed the door.

"Kingston," she blurted the same moment he said, "Vanessa."

"Please. Go on." He gestured for her to continue.

Summoning her courage, she clasped her hands and put forth what had been tormenting her for the past hour. "How will we convince anyone our marriage has not been consummated if we share a chamber?"

He cupped his nape and gave her a long, contemplative look, then veered his gaze to the bed, which dominated the chamber.

"Vanessa. May I speak plainly?"

"Of course." She nodded. "I'd prefer that you always do so."

"Yes, well…" He cleared his throat. "My parents always shared a chamber. My siblings will also expect that we do so. If we don't, their suspicions will be raised. That is one reason I suggested you stay at Woolpack

Inn."

So it hadn't only been to hide her away.

Or was it to protect her or protect his brothers and sisters?

"But they would've thought me pompous and haughty and that I believed myself above them had I done so." Likely, they already thought as much. "Kingston, you know what I'm saying is true."

"I'll concede there may be a degree of truth in what you say." His smile turned rueful as he skimmed that blue gaze over her appreciatively. "As for your worries about the annulment, a physician's examination can determine if your maidenhead is intact."

Flames scorched dual paths up her cheeks. "Oh."

"Forgive me for speaking bluntly, but there really is no delicate way to say it."

"I did ask you to." Vanessa hadn't expected that intimate revelation, however. Brushing a strand of hair off her forehead, she wandered to the room's other window.

"Vanessa, there is another reason I'm against us sharing a bedchamber."

"Oh?" She cocked her head, trying to discern what that might be.

Kingston's clear, penetrating blue, blue gaze revealed nothing.

He'd moved to stand directly before her, and Vanessa couldn't break eye contact with him. A current hummed between them, scintillating and mesmerizing, much like it had that first night.

"You see, wife," he said, drawing her slowly into the iron circle of his embrace, "I feared I'd do exactly what I'm doing now. You are a temptation I cannot resist."

He lowered his head and covered her mouth with his.

Vanessa wasn't sure what to expect, never having been kissed before. But it wasn't the spiral of heat and want swirling through her.

She clutched at his bulging arms and kissed him back. She wasn't sure if she was doing it correctly, but from his throaty groan and the way he gathered her closer to his chest, pressing his palms between her shoulder blades and at the small of her back, she must've done something right.

He teased the seam of her mouth with his tongue, seeking entrance. She parted her lips to his exploration, and every bone in her body turned to pudding. Or custard. Or jelly. Or some other pliable substance.

Loud, youthful male laughter boomed farther down the corridor, and Vanessa sprang away from him, holding her fingers across her swollen mouth.

Good God, what was she doing?

Kissing Kingston?

This wasn't part of the arrangement.

He tucked another wayward curl behind her ear.

She caught a whiff of his masculine scent, as tempting as any aphrodisiac, damn his eyes.

"You see why we cannot reside under the same roof, Nessa?"

Had he kissed her to make a point?

That she was so easily seduced or such a malleable ninny that all he had to do was look at her with that roguish grin tipping his mouth and his blue eyes smoldering, and she'd fall into his arms?

His bed?

Disappointment with herself at her weakness, and also with him for playing rakish tricks, wrapped around her heart. Anger licked her bruised pride no small amount too.

Kingston had deliberately used their mutual desire to *prove* their shared attraction.

It made Vanessa feel naive and stupid. And hurt.

She'd played right into his scheme, drat him.

Spinning away, she presented her back, afraid she'd say or do something imprudent.

Such as kiss him again?

No. *No*!

She'd not lose her head again. She would not.

"Tomorrow, I'll arrange rooms at the Woolpack Inn for you," he said quietly, a trace of defeat and regret in his rasping tone. "You can send your staff back to London."

Hugging her arms about herself, she stared out the window. "No."

"What?"

Vanessa faced him once more and shook her head.

"I said, no, Kingston. I'm not staying at the inn."

She wasn't some biddable servant or hireling to be shuffled off and sequestered away.

"I beg your pardon?" Thunder flashed in his blue eyes.

Vanessa filled her lungs and plunged onward, putting forth the suggestion that would solve all their problems. "Instead, I propose we move the entire household to Helmstead Gate."

10

"*Helmstead Gate?*" Kingston echoed, sounding like a blasted parrot again. Why did he do that with her? Turn into a witless cod pate?

"Yes." Vanessa nodded eagerly, an excited sparkle in her eyes.

Because she found Quail Hollow so lacking and couldn't wait to depart for her childhood home?

"There is plenty of room for everyone, including the servants." Her enthusiasm was a palatable thing. "And the refurbishing and renovating of Quail Hollow would commence much swifter if the house is unoccupied. Plus, there is a ballroom and music room, and I presume you'll want your siblings to, at the very least, learn to dance. And, quite naturally, there are other necessities. Their educations, for one.”

That mark hit home, an arrow straight to his heart, though he knew she hadn't intended to wound him.

Absorbed in her planning, Vanessa tapped her chin with her forefinger. “Of course, we'll need room for seamstresses and tailors for sewing and fittings. Then, there will be the various craftsmen and textile merchants, and they'll require room to display their wares. I'll have to send to London for paint and wallpaper samples too.”

Blast her for being so intrepid and logical.

Helmstead *would* be far better than Quail Hollow for all the reasons she mentioned and more.

She slid him a contemplative glance, a hint of hesitancy in her gaze. “Although, Kingston, I don't think there is any way we can avoid multiple trips to London for the larger household purchases and completion of your siblings' wardrobes.”

They'd only just arrived, and she was talking of returning to London?

He nearly shuddered at the abhorrent thought.

She was far braver than he, by God.

A journey to the city meant facing the gossip, tittering about his and Vanessa's rushed nuptials. He'd already heard there were bets on the books at Fortuna and White's that she was with child—not his child, the nasty chinwags—and had employed Mrs. Dorrian-Lane to find her a husband. The gossip rags had labeled him a skirt-snuffling fortune hunter, too.

But wasn't that precisely what Kingston *was* being?

Only he'd had the colossal good fortune of stumbling upon Vanessa—impossibly beautiful and innocent—at Fortuna, and like the selfish bastard he was, he'd seized the opportunity to spare himself humiliation and an undesirable stranger for a wife.

And yes, he'd do it again without a jot of hesitation for his family. Pride didn't put food on the table or a new roof on the house. Pride didn't make amends for his neglect and selfishness in the years since his parents' deaths.

"Your sisters and brothers can consider it a holiday of sorts."

They hadn't had a holiday since he'd put on his soldier's uniform and gallivanted off with a roguish wave and grin to prove himself a man. Then failed when it mattered the most.

He would not fail those he loved again.

Vanessa's exuberant prattling brought Kingston back to himself. Already, she'd shown herself kindly and caring to his brothers and sisters, even when her welcome had been less than cordial.

"And," she continued without missing a beat, her voice rising slightly as she warmed to the topic, "when Quail Hollow is restored, they'll return to a completely refurbished and finished house. As I'm sure you know, Kingston, construction and remodeling are trying, under the best of circumstances."

Which this most definitely was not—not by any overreach of the imagination.

"I believe residing at Helmstead would ease much tension, Kingston. It would also solve our bedchamber issue."

Of course, she was right.

Blast it all.

Kingston's concentration had been on the lands: planting crops and establishing a herd of prime cattle.

Well, and assuring the roof was repaired before winter set in. Wardrobes, lessons, and furnishings hadn't been his top priorities, though he conceded their importance.

Vanessa, however, had promptly identified the need for so much more than he had. If she was willing to oversee those things, that left him more time to focus on the estate becoming self-supportive. There were new farming methods he wanted to implement, though God knew he lacked any experience in such matters.

Regardless, numerous books had been authored on the subjects—he'd acquired several while in London—and other landed gentry had successfully introduced modern techniques.

Nonetheless, one uncomfortable thought niggled, wriggling around in his mind like an earthworm upon hot pavement. Just how much of his borrowed funds did Vanessa intend to spend on the other items she deemed necessities?

That was a discussion they must have sooner rather than later.

A mouse streaked across the floor before squeezing itself into a coin-sized hole between the wall and the floor. So absorbed in her planning, Vanessa hadn't noticed the terrified creature's hasty escape.

Kingston made a mental note.

Ridding the place of rodents was also a priority.

"It makes sense, Kingston. Helmstead is only half a mile away. We can renovate the entire house at once rather than room by room, which is what we'd have to do if Quail Hollow is occupied during the renovation. And it will save money too. The laborers' work won't be interrupted, which means they'll finish quicker."

She'd done it again. Faced facts straight on and made the most of the situation.

Just like at Fortuna.

There'd be no need for them to share a bedchamber either, thus removing the temptress standing a few feet away from his randy presence. Until now, his celibacy hadn't been an issue. Simply thinking of that day when Gabriel had died was enough to shrivel his bollocks. But from the moment he'd held Vanessa's hand in his at Fortuna, he'd sported a half-erection.

"What do you think?" Eyes wide and beseeching, Vanessa nibbled her thumbnail. *Her* sign of nervousness. "Would your brothers and sisters object to a temporary change in residence, or would they think me presumptuous?"

Yes, and yes.

At least Dorena and Gareth would think the latter.

Planting his hands on his hips and chin tucked to his chest, Kingston considered her proposal.

Would his brothers and sisters really balk?

To each having their own bedchamber?

No vermin or insects skittering about?

Heat throughout the house and servants to wait upon them? Not to mention plenty to eat and greater creature comforts than they'd had in a goodly while?

An idea sprang to mind.

He needn't move to Helmstead Gate, even if the rest of the family did.

"I'll agree to move the household to Helmstead Gate on the morrow, but I'll be staying here. To guard the place and to prevent any thievery of construction or other supplies."

That was a valid point she couldn't bring an argument against.

Vanessa's face fell, but a heartbeat later, she squared her shoulders and angled her chin upward. "That seems wise. It also provides us with a legitimate excuse to not share a bedchamber that won't give rise to speculation and gossip."

Her gaze slid to the bed, and a becoming flush stole up her face.

"We should probably go below. I'm sure dinner is nearly ready." She moved toward the door with the regal grace of a queen.

"Vanessa?"

Her fingers on the handle, she half-turned toward him. "Yes?"

In a few swift strides, he stood before her and cupped her shoulders. At once, the yearning to pull her into his embrace again engulfed him.

Kingston had vowed to God, to Gabriel, and to himself that he'd never again yield to passion's seducing allure.

"I shouldn't have kissed you, Nessa, but I don't regret it. I must, however, make certain it never happens again. I pledged an oath to you that I mean to keep. I never intended to marry, but circumstances made it a necessity. I want you to know that it isn't because I don't desire you or that I don't believe you would make an exceptional wife. However, I swore an oath some time ago that I cannot break."

What oath?

The unspoken question flashed in her eyes. Her mouth parted, and her warm honey gaze drifted to his lips.

Desire bolted through Kingston, and his pantaloons grew uncomfortably snug.

Placing her palm against his cheek, Vanessa bent her rosebud of a mouth into a tender smile.

God, how he wanted to turn his face and press his lips into her soft hand. To run the tip of his tongue over the creases and taste her.

"Lest you forget, I kissed you too, Kingston. I wanted to from that first night I saw you at Fortuna."

Had she felt that spark ignite between them too?

Vanessa rolled her shoulders, and Kingston released her.

"Now that our curiosity has been satisfied," she

said, "we can move forward with our original plan."

She sounded less than enthusiastic despite her composed proclamation.

Curiosity?

It was a bloody sight more than curiosity.

She pressed the latch, and as she stepped through the door frame, she said, "We both expect this union will be annulled, but it's a relief to know that if, God forbid, it cannot be, we would get on well together. We like and respect each other, and our kiss merely proves we are—*um*—compatible in other ways, too."

What a tame, wholly insufficient way to describe the conflagration that had erupted between them from that all-too-brief kiss. Vanessa had absolutely no idea how close she'd come to becoming his wife, in truth, a few minutes ago.

Kingston's heated blood still hummed with the want of her. To discover if she smelled of jasmine and verbena everywhere. The soft cleft of her elbow or behind her knees. The dimples of her lithe lower back. The ivory and rose of her breasts.

"Six months, Vanessa. Only half a year with no

additional attachments or complications."

Kingston deliberately kept any inflection out of his tone. This was a mutually beneficial arrangement as long as they adhered to the predetermined parameters.

That's horse shite, and you know it, Kingston Armond Joshua Kennedy Barclay.

It was true.

It had stopped being purely a business arrangement the instant Vanessa had floated into the drawing room on their wedding day. Even before that, if he were candid with himself. He'd *wanted* to marry her and claim Vanessa Becket as his own for now and always.

"Contracts are often amended," she ventured huskily, her guileless cognac gaze boring into his.

Not theirs.

Kingston couldn't take that chance, for he knew beyond a doubt that he'd take her to his bed and worship her body with his, perhaps even claim her heart, as his was well onto belonging to her.

The secret of what happened to Gabriel would forever be between them. He'd despise himself for not telling her the godawful truth. The dread, the genuine fear she'd leave and take any children they'd created together with her, would always stalk him like a dark phantom.

"I regret that's not possible. We'll adhere to what we agreed to, Vanessa. I shall concede to permit my family to reside at Helmstead Gate, but I'll sleep here."

Disappointment dulled the sparkle in her eyes, and he wavered, wanting to see that brilliant smile that warmed and soothed his soul.

"I shall also break my fast and sup with you," he conceded, needing to be near her despite his misgivings.

And *there* was that winsome smile. Swift and freely given, and his heart took to wing.

Stupid thing.

"But that is all I can compromise. We go our separate ways." He fisted his hands to keep from drawing her to him and pressing her head against his heart. "Trust me, Vanessa, when I tell you, it is for the best."

"You presume to know what is best for me?" A hint of pink touched her cheeks, but her smile remained in place, though sadness seeped into her eyes, turning them a deep umber. She gave a small shake of her head, and a curl that had escaped its confines fluttered by her ear.

"I'll see you below, Kingston. Never fear that I intend to renege on our *temporary* arrangement."

Jesus, how he loathed those last two words.

Unable to move, Kingston stood there, appreciating the gentle sway of her generous hips as she glided away, wishing she could be his for all time. And knowing he didn't deserve her. Could never have her.

Not after causing Gabriel's death.

Madeline stepped into the hallway, and arms crossed, glared at him, suspicion narrowing her blue eyes. "What, exactly, is going on, Kingston? Is Vanessa your wife or not?"

11

Helmstead Gate

Three and one-half weeks later

Vanessa hummed to herself as she applied a dab of perfume behind each ear in preparation for dinner. Bending her mouth into a naughty smile, she applied a drop between her breasts, too.

She wore a new gown—a shimmering green-blue affair with silver threads woven into the material—that reminded her of a warm breeze blowing across the ocean's surface on a summer day. The unique fabric changed color depending on the light, and she'd never seen anything quite like it.

Choosing to wear the gown tonight had nothing to

do with her desire to impress Kingston or the new course she'd decided upon this very afternoon.

Liar, chided her bothersome but rational self.

Fine, she *did* want to see the glow of masculine appreciation in his eyes when he saw her in the garment.

Was that so very wrong?

They were husband and wife, after all.

Yes, but Vanessa *was* trying to change the terms of their agreement.

Indeed, she was.

For, the truth of it was she'd come to an irrefutable conclusion: There could be no better husband for her than Kingston. Not in ten lifetimes. And since she only had one life, she intended to seduce her husband.

Patient and kind with his family, Kingston was also quick to smile, give praise and encouragement, and on occasion, tease. Even she wasn't immune from his playful jesting, which wrinkled the corners of his eyes in a disarming fashion.

If he wasn't so dashed pleasing to the eye or didn't send her pulse and heart into a fitful rhythm each time they were together, she might've been able to resist him and her growing feelings toward him.

For a man who'd known the horrors of war, he'd not barricaded his emotions behind an impenetrable wall. Truth be told, he wasn't the least afraid to show his affection. His sisters received a hello kiss each morning and a farewell hug and kiss to their foreheads every evening. He'd grasp his brothers' hands in a firm handshake as he pulled them in for a warm embrace, too.

Already, Vanessa's servants adored him, and if there was a single merchant or laborer who had cause to find fault with Kingston, she'd not heard a whisper of it.

In short, he was everything she could desire in a mate.

Several times, Vanessa had caught a wistful glint in his eyes as he roved his gaze over her and his family when he bid them all good night.

He wanted to stay.

She could see the longing and desire in those blue depths, yet he held himself in restraint. Although she respected and admired his discipline in rigidly sticking to their marriage terms, she wished he wasn't *quite* so honorable.

That smoldering kiss…

Vanessa curled her toes into her satin slippers as a delicious shudder rippled across her bare shoulders, and she touched a fingertip to her lips. When she closed her eyes, she could still feel his warm, soft, smooth mouth upon hers.

Who knew a man's mouth could evoke such ardent sensations?

Such all-consuming feelings?

She'd relived every moment of that delicious melding of their mouths each night as she lay in her lonely bed, staring up at the ceiling and listening to the sounds a house makes at night. With each recollection, she'd fallen a little bit more in love with Kingston. Oh, she'd attempted to caution her foolish heart to cease with such girlish silliness until, at last, she stopped doing so.

In the still, dark hours of the night, Vanessa had come to realize an indisputable truth: the heart had a will of its own when it came to whom it chose to love.

And hers had picked Kingston Barclay. Former

soldier. Future duke. Guardian to five delightful siblings.

Her husband.

Shaking out her skirts iridescent folds, she smiled, well pleased with the overall effect. Denying the fluttering in her tummy was anything other than nerves would make her a liar. It was a far better thing to take a risk on a grand adventure with him as her spouse than play it safe and wonder what could have been.

And so, she donned this bold confection of a gown, hoping to drive her unsuspecting husband out of his mind with desire.

Except for her wedding day and her purple traveling costume, tonight was the first time she'd worn bright colors. Vanessa squared her shoulders and gave her head a little toss of defiance. This was a new chapter in her life, and by continuing to wear mourning weeds, she only reminded herself of her losses.

One had a choice in this life: to look to the future and embrace whatever joy and happiness it might hold, or stay stuck in the past with all its sorrows and regrets, which far too often morphed into bitterness and resentment.

Vanessa had chosen the former and hoped—Lord above how she hoped—to convince Kingston to do the same with her. To remain married and experience life's pleasures and burdens together.

They complimented each other in so many ways.

How could she not love the man her brother had deemed his best friend since they were in short pants? And if Kingston could love Gabriel as he had, why couldn't he also come to love Vanessa?

Allowing her eyelids to drift shut, she envisioned holding a chubby, fair-haired boy with his father's blue eyes and contagious smile. She'd like lots of babies—Kingston's children.

For over three weeks, Kingston had been pleasant, cordial even, but he treated her in the manner a wizened monk or ancient eunuch would have done. He only touched her when absolutely necessary and only as briefly as politesse dictated. It was almost as if he didn't trust himself, and tonight, she meant to put that theory to the test.

With the help of this gown, a new hairstyle, and a

little harmless flirtation. Well, perhaps not so innocuous flirtation. Vanessa did want to succeed in enticing her handsome husband into her bed, after all.

These past days had been a whir of continuous activity. The expected journey to London had not manifested as she simply hadn't had the time. Between refurbishing Quail Hollow, overseeing Helmstead Gate, numerous shopping excursions, and everything else that went along with transforming her new siblings' lives, she'd scarcely had time to pen a letter to her dearest friends, Rayne, Duchess of Kincade, and Everleigh, Duchess of Sheffield.

Though slightly older than Vanessa, both women had been unfailingly kind to her and had become as close as sisters.

Gabriel had been eight years her senior, and after he'd joined the army and while Owen was off being a wastrel, she'd felt much like an only child. The truth of it was that Vanessa wasn't accustomed to the almost constant commotion that commenced with having five young people about. Make that five young people, two energetic Dalmatian puppies, and six romping kittens.

Grinning, she shook her head.

It was a delightful sort of chaos.

Originally, Vanessa had acquired the dogs as her pets, but Paxton and Gareth had formed such immediate and emotional bonds with them that she'd decided to wait to obtain a dog for herself. Besides, the six kittens were always in some sort of mischief.

Dorena could be credited with the latter. She'd found the mewling litter alone and unattended in the stables. Either their mother had abandoned them, or more likely, she'd met an unfortunate end.

Dorena had insisted on mothering the foundlings. Such a transformation had occurred in Vanessa's youngest sister-in-law as she cared for the little orange, white, and black puffs of fur that it was hard to believe that three short weeks ago, she'd been starchy and unfriendly.

Vanessa's friendship with Madeline had blossomed once more, and Rebecca had become a dear friend, too. Her impish brothers-in-law, still a bit shy and awkward around her, had won Vanessa's affections, as had the slightly more taciturn Dorena.

Whenever Vanessa's thoughts migrated to September when her time with the Barclays was to end—and they invariably did—she ruthlessly quashed them. Instead of regretting that nearly a month had already passed, she instead elected to be optimistic.

Five months remained in which to woo her husband.

Every now and again, she'd catch Madeline watching her, a contemplative expression on her pretty face before she'd whisk it away and replace her reverie with a bright smile. And inevitably, Vanessa wondered if her sister-in-law questioned why the newlyweds not only didn't share a bedchamber but also didn't even sleep under the same roof.

Oh, the excuses Kingston supplied were viable, if not entirely convincing.

"There's too much risk in leaving the house unattended," he'd declared while glancing at his timepiece as if he couldn't wait to depart. After snapping the pocket watch closed and returning it to his waistcoat, he'd scratched his nose. "Someone might steal the construction materials or sneak into the house and, finding it uninhabited, ransack the place."

"Couldn't servants be assigned to guard Quail Hollow?" Dorena had asked when informed of the living arrangements, her keen gaze suspicious as it drifted between her brother and Vanessa.

"No. They are needed here," Kingston stated firmly. "Vanessa has a stepbrother who would do her harm." He'd looked to each of his brothers and sisters in turn, and Madeline's eyes had gone round as if she'd suddenly comprehended something.

Did she suspect he'd married Vanessa to protect her?

"She is part of our family now," he said without glancing at Vanessa. "And we protect our own, don't we?"

How Vanessa wished he meant more—felt more than those practical words conveyed. Nevertheless, tears had stung her eyes as the Barclays had heartily affirmed their support.

Even Dorena.

That had been the first night at Helmstead Gate, and no one had questioned him since.

However, tonight, the tide was about to change.

Vanessa wiped suddenly damp palms down the front of her gown.

No more demurely nodding a pleasant good night and watching Kingston depart for Quail Hollow before seeking her lonely chamber. Or, as he had on several occasions, closeting himself in Helmstead's study to deal with business and estate matters since Quail Hollow's was gutted at present.

At least the new roof was completed, and according to Kingston, any small, furry, crawly things that had once made the house their home had been sent on their way.

Having a soft heart toward all God's creatures, Vanessa hadn't inquired as to precisely what that meant.

Still gazing into the long glass, she rotated side to side, admiring the way the gown's folds swished around her ankles. Never before had she felt so elegant or attractive. She was glad she'd let Madeline talk her into purchasing this fabric and suspected her sister-in-law was playing fairy godmother or matchmaker.

A small frown crimped Vanessa's mouth as she

considered her revealing decolletage. Possessing a neckline a trifle lower than she was accustomed to, the bodice emphasized her generous breasts swelling above the bodice. She'd seen far more skin exposed in London, but she'd never dared be so bold herself.

Canterbury proved to be a tremendous resource, and while the shops weren't as prestigious as those on Bond Street, they'd been more than sufficient to outfit the six Barclay siblings in a manner that would no longer cause them chagrin.

Kingston fussed and huffed that he didn't need any new clothes, but Vanessa had said if he refused to be fitted, she'd simply take his old clothes to the tailor. She needn't have worried her husband was a fortune hunter.

The man could stretch a coin farther than anyone she'd ever met, and he made her feel quite the spendthrift when she'd always considered herself quite frugal and wise with funds.

True, she'd spent a considerable amount to date. However, considering how insufficient the Barclays' wardrobes had been and the need to replace practically everything at Quail Hollow, she thought she'd done quite well economizing.

Kingston needn't know that Vanessa only showed him a portion of the invoices and bills. Naturally, after the tension of renovating was finished, she'd reveal all. She wouldn't keep secrets from her husband.

For certain, a few weeks in London were in order before Madeline's and Rebecca's come out. Nevertheless, there was plenty of time to prepare for that momentous occasion.

Gareth and Paxton required proper togs for Harrow—their choice of school next year.

Dorena's wardrobe would also need expanding before she attended Mrs. Avelina Crablace's School for Young Ladies—also her decision because of the institution's emphasis on the sciences.

Nonetheless, there was no rush as the three youngest Barclays wouldn't start instruction for a few months yet. It was too late to enroll them this year. This meant they had the whole summer before them, and Vanessa had many pleasant outings and events planned. Once the current bustle subsided, that was.

This morning, during her daily after-breakfast

meeting with Kingston in the study, Vanessa had insisted on sponsoring Madeline's and Rebecca's Seasons. Quite naturally, if she did so, it would be most unfair to not also pay for the boys' and Dorena's tuition, as well as other expenses required for their education.

Kingston had been less than receptive to the suggestions.

Vanessa had also broached the subject of assuming the financial burden for an additional wing at Quail Hollow. After all, shouldn't those with plenty do for those who lacked?

Kingston had strenuously objected, stating his family unequivocally would not abuse Vanessa's generous nature. However, his argument had been cut short when the slight of frame but garish of attire—*burnt orange, squash yellow, and fuchsia were never meant to be worn together, except perhaps as bird feathers*—Monsieur LeTessier arrived for his thrice-weekly dance instruction.

"This conversation is *not* over, Vanessa. We shall finish it tonight," Kingston had gritted out, lowering his head to speak directly into her ear lest any nearby servant overhear their exchange.

Instead of being shocked or peeved at the intensity of his tone, she'd only been able to focus on the warmth of his breath teasing her ear and how utterly delicious he smelled.

Shaving lather. Horse. Leather. And a hint of mint.

Gazing into the cheval mirror, Vanessa adjusted a curl, and at last, satisfied with her appearance, she left her bedchamber. Not, however, before casting a longing glance toward the door leading to what should've been the gentlemen of the house's chamber.

Soon, she promised herself.

Soon, Kingston, we will truly be man and wife.

Three hours later

Through half-closed eyes, Kingston observed his wife as, amidst much laughter and light-hearted jesting, she played whist with Madeline, Gareth, and Rebecca. Dorena occupied herself with her rambunctious kittens, and Paxton lay upon the floor before the hearth, reading *Gulliver's Travels*.

The boy had his nose in one book or another since moving to Helmstead Gate and availing himself of the substantial library. Remus and Romulus, the fat Dalmatian puppies with their needle-like teeth, *finally* slept on either side of him.

Kingston's boots sported several scratches and

teeth marks where the little beasts had gleefully chewed upon his footwear when he'd sat down this evening—precisely why he hadn't worn the new pair of Hessians delivered last week. Hessians he had no knowledge of until they'd been presented by his wife, two bright patches of color on her porcelain cheeks.

He suspected she was of the opinion it was better to ask forgiveness for overstepping rather than permission. A grin pulled the edges of his mouth upward. And by Jove, he couldn't bring himself to be perturbed by her audacity.

The daring little minx.

Vanessa reported that in the past fortnight, no less than two and forty items, from shoes to rugs to plants—even a feather duster and three baskets—had met gruesome fates due to the spotted terrors presently curled into fat, slumbering little balls.

Kingston couldn't recall ever feeling so content himself.

No, not content, per se.

In point of fact, his unappeased sexual desires didn't lend for any degree of peacefulness or serenity.

He was randy as a stag in the rut. He shifted slightly, grateful his crossed legs hid the hard bulge of his arousal.

A small groan escaped him, and Madeline speared him a keen, inquisitive look.

As if he'd choked on his brandy, he pretended to cough behind his hand.

The corners of her eyes flexed.

She wasn't having any of it.

Bollocks.

He lifted his tumbler in a mocking salute before taking a healthy swig of the spirit. It was good stuff—a superior French cognac. He was fairly certain Vanessa purchased it, as well as the other quality spirits, for his enjoyment.

Another piece of his heart fell at her dainty feet.

She'd been slowly chipping away at the hardened organ since offering to become his bride at Fortuna. It wouldn't be long until she owned the entire thing lock, stock, and barrel. If she didn't already.

He studied the amber liquid, marveling at her consideration. No one else in the household partook of strong spirits, and to his knowledge, Helmstead Gate had not been overrun with gentleman callers.

She'd done it for him.

His attention traveled to his two oldest sisters. They were of marriageable age, and the thought of them entering into an arranged marriage or a marriage of convenience soured his stomach. He'd do everything within his power to ensure they married for love as their parents had.

As Vanessa should have done.

More on point, Kingston had benefited from their union far more than she had, and yet not one word of complaint had passed her lips. Lips that were almost always arranged in a pleasant half-smile as if she were truly happy and content with her situation.

When Madeline had confronted him about his marriage to Vanessa, he'd told her the truth. His sister was too intelligent to believe a happily married couple, especially newlyweds, would not share a bedchamber.

"Oh, Kingston. I fear you will both come to regret what you've done," was all she'd said.

However, at this very moment, her winged blonde

eyebrows were arched high in an, *I'm on to you* look.

He'd been too obvious in ogling his delectable wife.

Madeline covertly slid Vanessa a considering glance, but she seemed unaware of Kingston's gawping.

Her lower lip caught between her teeth, his wife tapped the fingertips of one hand upon the table.

She was a horrid player.

Her expression gave her away every time.

She leaned forward, and her decolletage swelled invitingly.

His mouth went dry as Egypt's hot, arid air.

That bloody, tantalizing gown.

With every movement, the blasted thing begged him to strip it from Vanessa and reveal the lush treasures the fabric hid from his scorching gaze—the treasures he yearned to explore at his leisure.

For the rest of their lives.

When Kingston had arrived this evening, he'd been wholly entranced.

He'd craned his neck so hard to see a full glimpse of her as she stood by the window chatting with Rebecca that he'd nearly plowed into the mahogany, marble-topped table beside the drawing room doorway. As it was, he'd let slip a curse as he lunged to catch a tottering vase—no doubt a very expensive vase—before it crashed to the floor.

When he'd glanced up, everyone in the room stared at him, and by God, there'd been the merest gratified hint of a smile at the corners of Vanessa's mouth.

The minx.

He'd be bound that she knew exactly what effect the gown would have on him.

What game did the vixen play now?

Casting a reluctant glance at the gold and green marble ormolu mantle clock, with its trio of irritatingly cheerful, naked mythical creatures, he sighed.

Half nine.

He'd already lingered an extra half an hour with his family past his typical departure time to either return to Quail Hollow House or adjourn to Helmstead Gate's study. A stack of invoices in need of reviewing, supply orders, and correspondences he'd already neglected for several days awaited him there.

And yet, averse to disturbing the tableau of domestic tranquility before him, he delayed his departure. His siblings' hollow cheeks had filled out, and their youthful faces now shone with health instead of worry, hunger, and fatigue. There could be no doubt Vanessa was good for them, as had living at Helmstead Gate.

They, too, were happy.

It was Paxton who broke the peaceful ambiance. Yawning, he closed his book and climbed to his feet. "We have an early morning riding lesson on the morrow, so I'll bid you goodnight."

Attired in a neat walnut brown suit, he actually bent into a perfectly proper bow.

Yes, Vanessa had worked wonders in a very short time. But then, Kingston had known she would. She had that innate ability. To bring out the best in people.

Even him.

Elligon seemed the sole exception, but that blackguard was a greedy, self-centered bugger. At least the sod had made no further attempts to harass Vanessa. However, that didn't mean Kingston let his guard down.

He'd privately spoken to each male staff member and explained they needed to be diligent and notify him if anything unusual occurred. Vanessa's servants were devoted to her, and each had assured him they would guard her with their lives.

Grinning at Paxton, Kingston lifted a finger from his glass and pointed it at his youngest brother. "Very wise of you, and that bow was worthy of a courtier. Well done, you."

Paxton beamed under his praise.

Kingston appreciated that his brothers and sisters hadn't balked at their seven o'clock riding lessons. But then, none had been slugabeds prior to moving to their more luxurious accommodations, either. They were accustomed to rising early and hard work.

"Yes, we should retire, as well." Smiling her agreement, Rebecca laid down her cards. "We've appointments in Canterbury tomorrow afternoon, too."

More gowns? Hats? Slippers? Fripperies?

He couldn't begrudge their fun, yet neither did he want Vanessa to assume those financial obligations. It made him feel guilty as hell that he couldn't provide for his family—made him feel like a bloody fortune hunter indeed.

And, the truth was that until he inherited the duchy, there was bloody little he could do to alter that except to turn a profit with his lands. Even then, it would be years before he could repay Vanessa.

"I confess, I'm quite done in. I'm sure you are too, Vanessa, as you were up with the chickens this morn," Madeline said, the merest thread of puckishness coloring her voice. The bland stare she leveled Kingston didn't fool him.

His oldest sister was up to something.

Startled, Vanessa glanced at the clock. The candles' glow played across her hair, giving her an ethereal radiance.

"Goodness. Is that truly the time?" A wide smile wreathed her mouth as she accepted a kitten from Dorena and nuzzled the calico's neck. "Good company tends to make time fly, doesn't it?"

Gareth also stood. "Come, Remus. Romulus."

With a snap of his fingers, the two puppies yawned and rose, obediently staring up at him. Their pure white tails thumped upon the pink, burgundy, and green Aubusson carpet. A carpet they'd each *anointed* several times.

"Such are the hazards of having puppies," Vanessa had said last night as a pair of dutiful maids had mopped up the most recent accident.

A few more moments passed as goodnights were exchanged. Remus and Romulus, plump as piglets, scampered after Paxton and Gareth while his sisters, each carrying two kittens, slowly drifted from the room. Madeline gave him an impish smile as she shut the door firmly behind her.

Only the fireplace's popping and snapping and the clock's *tick-tock, tick-tock* interrupted the weighty silence that descended upon the drawing room. Vanessa made no effort to follow Kingston's brothers and sisters, as was her wont.

Instead, she tidied the cards and put them away.

The air crackled with tension and electricity as if a bolt of lightning were about to strike at any moment.

Kingston should go.

He scratched his nose and, upon realizing what he

was doing, promptly laid his hand on the chair's arm.

It was the height of folly to remain.

Forcing himself to rise, he cupped his nape and stared into the capering flames. He'd not last another five months of keeping Vanessa at a distance. Of that, he was certain. Perhaps it would be best not to come every day anymore and only check in once weekly.

Even as the thought crossed his mind, he discarded it.

He would not leave his siblings care to Vanessa. She'd already taken on most of the burden, he was chagrined to admit. And he'd not have his brothers and sisters think he cared so little for them that he couldn't be bothered to visit when Quail Hollow was but half a mile away.

Guilt hollowed his gut at the years of neglect they'd already suffered.

Closing his eyes, Kingston summoned every bit of resolve he possessed.

Go. Leave. Now.

"Kingston?"

His eyes flew open.

Vanessa stood only inches away, her brandy-colored eyes luminous with some emotion he couldn't identify.

How had she moved so swiftly and silently?

Or was it that he'd been so absorbed in his rueful ruminations he hadn't heard her?

Her tongue peeked out and touched the corner of her red mouth.

A groan lodged in his throat.

He wanted to touch that sweet, delicate corner with *his* tongue.

Saints above, Kingston's mouth went dry as chalk again as lust pounded through him with the force of stampeding elephants. An immense battle fulminated within him. Two sides wrestling for dominance, cleaving him in two. Each convinced their course was best.

For her.

For him.

Take her. She's your wife.

Only for a short time.

It wouldn't be fair to either of us.

She wants you, too.

She did.

God curse Kingston for a raffish scoundrel. He'd been with enough women to recognize feminine longing. And the incandescent glow in Vanessa's beautiful eyes, tender and yearning, told him all that he needed to know.

But this was Vanessa.

Gabriel's sister.

A woman unlike any other. Still, as sexually experienced as Kingston was, foreign vulnerability and doubt wreaked havoc on his confidence because sex with her would never be just physical gratification.

Stepping nearer until her slippers touched his boots, her iridescent skirts brushed his black evening trousers. She laid a slim-fingered hand upon his forearm. "This morning, you said you wanted to finish our discussion."

Ah, that was why she'd lingered.

Disillusionment curled bitterly in the pit of his stomach.

Vanessa merely wanted to assure herself he'd not forbid her to finance even more than she already had.

More fool him. Kingston had wished she'd stayed because she was as disinclined to part his company as he was hers.

Vanessa's position afforded him a splendid view of the mouthwatering valley between her rising and falling breasts. His groin swelled with burgeoning want and need for this woman, and he ran his knuckles gently over her satiny cheek.

Her eyes and mouth went soft. Inviting. Tempting as sin, and God knew he was no saint.

Perhaps their unfinished discussion wasn't the only reason she'd lingered.

"Kingston," she whispered, her tone throaty, her hand tightening on his arm. Then she utterly flummoxed him by rising on tiptoe and pressed her petal-soft mouth to his.

Kingston was lost.

The last shred of his waning willpower splintered into a million sparkling pieces. With a guttural groan, he hauled her into his embrace, claiming her lips in a searing kiss. There was nothing tender about this meshing of their mouths. Raw hunger compelled him, drove him to brand Vanessa as his.

Twining her arms around his neck, she opened her mouth beneath his sensual onslaught. Their tongues mated in an age-old replica of what he desperately wanted to do with his body. They dueled and parried, and with each little sigh or mewl that escaped her, he grew marble hard and impossibly harder still.

Kingston had known women before.

He'd bedded dozens, but nothing had ever been like this all-consuming, inexplicable, permeating need for Vanessa. Intimacy with other women had been purely carnal—a physical necessity, much like breathing or sleeping or satiating one's hunger or thirst.

But this….

Whatever *this* was, it was so much, much more. His need for her came from the depths of his very soul, and that frightened the hell out of him even as it drove him onward.

"Vanessa," he moaned, nuzzling her neck and inhaling her jasmine and verbena perfume. For as long as he lived, he'd associate those scents with her.

On a lengthy, ragged sigh, her head fell back,

exposing the long, graceful length of her ivory throat as she clung to him.

"Kingston, please." Whimpering, Vanessa clutched at his shoulders.

The pounding of his heart thrummed a steady, erotic tempo.

Vanessa. Vanessa. Vanessa.

Gasping for breath, Kingston rested his forehead against hers, battling to find a single thread of self-control. He must stop before it was too late. There'd be no going back if he made love to her.

Once more, lust would seal his fate. And someone else's, too. Someone he cared for very much. But this mysterious, inexpressible thing was more—*holy Jesus, so much more*—than mere lust.

"Kingston, I want you," she moaned.

Ah, hell.

He'd known the moment Vanessa kissed him that he was lost. She consumed him, his desire a conflagration in his soul, an inferno he couldn't extinguish. Nor, quite honestly, did he wish to.

So they'd consummate their vows. Stay married.

There were far, far worse things than being married to this nymph.

At that moment, he couldn't bring himself to regret what they were about to do. For certain, self-castigation would scourge him later.

Bending, he scooped Vanessa into his arms. As he carried her to the settee, she placed hot little kisses over his jaw and neck.

He chuckled, genuine joy burgeoning in him.

His wife was a hot-blooded little spitfire.

Letting her slide to her feet, he framed her face between his palms and peered into her eyes. "If we do this, Nessa, there is no going back."

Going back?

Was Kingston mad?

Vanessa wanted this with every part of her being. Wanted to make love with her husband. She had, in all honesty, since he'd kissed her that first time almost a month ago.

No, before that.

When she'd exited the alcove at Fortuna and seen him standing there, all majestic, tantalizing maleness.

She appreciated this meant that there would be no annulment, and she reveled in the knowledge just as she would rejoice in their joining.

To remain married to this enigmatic, remarkable man.

To bear his children.

Oh, God, yes. Yes.

"I know, Kingston." Tears stung behind her closed eyelids. "I know."

Vanessa loved him. She needed to show him with her body what she couldn't say with words just yet.

"Are you absolutely positive, love?" He rubbed his thumb over her swollen lower lip, and she playfully bit it.

"I want this, Kingston. I want you."

Then, before he could object and rather amazed at her boldness, she shimmied out of her gown, leaving her standing before him in only her stays, stockings, and slippers. She supposed she ought to be embarrassed, but instead, she felt empowered.

Bold. Daring. Seductive.

"My God, you are exquisite, Nessa." As Kingston took her in, his gaze traveling the length of her in a sensual, visual caress, his eyes darkened to navy blue. "Perfection. A goddess."

"Then why don't you worship me with your body?" she teased.

"Oh, make no mistake, love. I intend to." His voice deepened to a low, husky rasp. "And then you'll be mine."

"Yes. Make me yours, Kingston."

With a growl, he shucked his coat and shirt in rapid succession.

She licked her lower lip and laid her palms on his chest, running her fingers through the soft mat of springy hair there. Letting her curiosity guide her, she trailed her fingertips lower, over the stairsteps of his torso, smiling to herself as his sinewy muscles quivered beneath her touch.

He was sculpted, molded, masculine perfection.

When she hesitated at the waistband of his trousers, suddenly uncertain, he covered her hand. "I'll do that." His throaty timbre rasped across her, causing a little shiver of scorching desire to tingle its way over her raised flesh.

Good Lord, such unfamiliar heat singed her that she might very well burst into flames.

"You lie down." He jerked his chin toward the settee.

They were truly going to do this. In the drawing room. On the settee. Where anyone might come upon them.

Hopefully, the closed door ought to deter all but the most impertinent.

To hide her nervousness as Kingston stripped away the last of his clothing, Vanessa presented her back, concentrating on removing her stays with trembling fingers. She wasn't quite brave enough to watch him disrobe. She'd just kicked off her slippers and reached to untie the ribbon holding her stocking when he came up behind her and rested his hand over hers.

"Leave them."

The hard contours of his torso and chest pressed into her shoulder blades, the curly hair tickling her.

They were a symphony of contrasts.

Creamy and sun-bronzed. Firm and soft. Rounded and lean.

She gasped.

"Easy," Kingston whispered into her hair, grazing his rough fingertips over her shoulders as if easing a skittish horse.

Her heart settled into its proper place once more, anticipation replacing her disquiet.

After rotating her to face him, he began pulling the pins from her hair.

She ran her fingertips experimentally over the hard, puckered scars covering his back and shoulders.

How he must've suffered.

When he'd tossed aside the last hairpin, Kingston fanned her hair over her bare shoulders and chest. Catching a strand between his thumb and forefinger, he rubbed the tendril.

"I adore your hair, love. It's spun moonbeams."

Kingston brushed his mouth over hers, flicking his tongue out to lick the seam of her lips.

In a deft move, he laid her upon the settee and angled himself beside her. Brushing a hand over her face, he stared into her eyes. Eyes so full of tenderness that it brought a rush of moisture to hers.

Lord, how she loved this man.

"You only have to tell me, and I vow I'll stop. We won't do anything you don't wish to, Vanessa."

"I told you, Kingston. I *want* this." Curving her

mouth into a tender smile, she pressed her lips to the pulse jumping at the juncture of his throat. "I want to remain your wife."

He looked at her for a long, compelling moment, his gaze inscrutable, and Vanessa knew he fought an inner battle.

Would he choose them?

A future together, forever and always?

Please, God.

He must, for she didn't know how she'd live without him now that he'd burrowed his way into her heart.

"You are an unqualified wonder, Mrs. Barclay."

Understanding dawned, and joy winged through her.

Then Kingston's hands and mouth were everywhere, all at once.

"I love you, Vanessa."

14

Kingston hadn't meant to tell Vanessa that which he'd only recently acknowledged to himself. He'd never have done so had they not consummated their vows. And since she'd be his until he drew his last breath, he'd wanted her to know.

"I love you, Vanessa." Closing his eyes, happiness humming through him, he pressed his lips to her forehead, branding her as his. "You have made me so very, very happy."

He lowered his attention, raking his gaze over every detail of her beloved face.

A tear slid from the corner of one of her eyes, then another and another. With a ragged sob, she buried her face in his shoulder and clung to him.

His brave, intrepid Vanessa, who'd only ever been stoic, shuddered against him as she wept.

"And I…love you…too," came her stilted, watery reply.

Thank God.

For a few horrible, agonizing seconds, terror had gripped Kingston.

Whispering endearments, he held her until her tears subsided, and, sniffling, she raised her gaze to meet his. Her eyelashes spikey from her weeping, a tremulous smile played across her swollen mouth. "I believe this means we shan't seek an annulment."

"No, minx." Tweaking her nose, he grinned. "We assuredly will not."

She sniffled again, and he reached to retrieve his handkerchief from his coat pocket. "Here."

"Thank you," came her muffled voice as she wiped her damp face. She blew her nose and, after folding the cloth and tucking it behind her, gave him a shy look.

With her hair tousled, bright spots of color on her cheeks, and her lips cherry red from his kisses, she'd never looked more beautiful or tempting. And now she was truly his.

"I shall make you happy, Vanessa."

Kingston would keep that vow, but first, he must tell her the truth.

She kissed his chest, and love blossomed behind his breastbone, so rich and powerful that tears stung his eyes.

"I'm already ecstatically happy, Kingston."

The fire burned low, and a chill permeated the room. Reaching over her, he pulled the seafoam green knitted throw from the back of the settee. After draping it across their naked forms, he settled her into the cradle of his arms. Several blissful, contented moments passed, only their even breathing, the fire's occasional crackle, and the clock's hypnotic *tick-tock* breaking the serenity.

"Darling, there's something I must tell you." Kingston should've done so before making love to her. Should've given her the right to choose whether she'd stay with him after she learned the ugly details of Gabriel's death.

If she decided not to, he'd let her go, of course. And when he became the Duke of Caerleon, he'd use his power to seek a dissolution of their marriage, though it would rip his heart from his chest and see it pulverized beneath a thousand horses' hooves.

Tilting her head back, Vanessa searched his face. "What is it?"

"I want you to know the truth about Gabriel's death." Taking one of her slender hands, Kingston pressed his mouth to the knuckles.

She swallowed and gave a small nod, a tinge of uncertainty in her expression. "All right."

The brave darling.

Of course, she'd face that straight on, too.

As Kingston brushed his fingertips over her silky shoulders and back, every now and again, pressing a tender kiss into her fragrant hair, he told her all. Kingston didn't spare himself, laying the blame precisely where it belonged—at his feet.

"It should have been me that died that day, Vanessa. Not Gabriel."

He stared up at the ceiling, watching the shadows play across the ornate surface painted with cherubim capering amongst clouds.

Though he'd considered himself a brave soldier and had never once shrunk from duty in cowardice, Kingston couldn't bring himself to look at her. To see the condemnation and perhaps hatred in her honey gaze.

She remained perfectly still and utterly silent for a full one-hundred and sixteen *tick-tocks* of the cursed clock. With every passing second, his heart sank further, his hope evaporating.

"Kingston?" Vanessa's tone didn't hold any of the wrath and accusation he'd expected. Deserved, truth be told.

Bracing himself, he brought his gaze to meet hers, expecting the worse.

"Would Gabriel have done the same for you?"

"What?" He wrinkled his forehead.

What did she mean?

"Would Gabriel have asked me to deliver a letter so that he might carry out an…assignation?" How did one delicately refer to a courtesan with one's wife?

Vanessa nodded, her fingers gripping the edge of the throw. Eyes wide, she roved her attention his face.

"He would have done." Kingston didn't doubt it for

an instant. That instance wasn't the first time they'd traded favors so that one of them might dally with a particularly fetching and willing woman.

"Without hesitation?" she pressed.

"Yes."

That had been the nature of their friendship. Kingston would've done nearly anything for Gabriel, and the reverse was also true.

"Then why, Kingston, do you continue to blame yourself for his death?"

He stared at her so dumbfounded that words escaped him.

Why?

Why?

"Because it *should* have been *me*, Vanessa," he rasped, anguish tearing at his heart. "It is my fault he is dead."

"No. It's not." Again, she shook her head, those silky strands brushing his arm as she laid her palm upon his chest, over his racing heart. "None of us has any control over the evil deeds of others. Nor do any of us know what each day will bring. And knowing Gabriel, he would not want you to continue to torment yourself."

"Vanessa..." Kingston despised the broken, pleading tenor in his voice.

"Forgive yourself, my love." She raised up and brushed her mouth across his. "I forgive you, though I do not believe you did wrong. However, I know you need to hear it from me."

She forgave him?

Did that mean...

"You'll stay with me and be my wife?" Rising above her, Kingston cupped her jaw, emotion choking him. Afraid he'd heard wrong, he asked, "You'll not leave?"

A tender smile curved Vanessa's mouth as she reached up and circled her arms behind his back, drawing him to her. "I'll never leave you, my darling. I love you."

When he made love to her that time, he vowed their very spirits and souls melded together. And when they reached the zenith together this time, his tears mixed with hers.

This was true, unconditional love.

Epilogue

Number Fourteen Berkeley Square, London
Late evening, May 1817

Vanessa bent her neck as Kingston unclasped the sapphire and diamond pendant, his Christmas gift to her, along with matching earrings. "I suspected Madeline and Rebecca would be a success, but I didn't expect they'd take London by storm." She chuckled as she removed the sparkling earrings. "Only out a fortnight, and they've each received multiple proposals."

"You don't suppose having a substantial dowry and a newly titled duke as a brother has anything to do with that, do you?" Kingston replied dryly, leaning over to place a kiss on her nape.

As always, her body hummed in response. She'd never tire of his touch and still thrilled that this man was her husband.

My dearest duke.

She turned and faced him, giving him a mock scold.

"For shame, Kingston. They are beautiful, witty, and intelligent young women. Yes, no doubt the dowries and your title have lured a fortune hunter or two—"

"Some claim *I* was a fortune hunter, and look how well that turned out." He waggled his eyebrows in that deliciously wicked way he had, and she couldn't suppress a giggle.

"*Pshaw.* You were no such thing." She arched an eyebrow. "I'll remind you that there were nasty gossips who said I was an upstart who bought a title with my fortune. Never mind that your uncle died within three months of our wedding, and you repaid every cent, plus interest."

That had been their first real heated argument. Vanessa had been highly affronted and refused to accept the money. At last, they'd agreed to put the funds in a trust for their children.

Kingston pulled her into his embrace, smashing her bosom against his chest and causing the sapphire and diamond pendant she'd pinned there to press into the tender flesh.

"Ouch."

"Forgive me, love." At once, Kingston released her. Sliding his long fingers into her decolletage, he grinned roguishly as he unpinned the gem. "You never did tell me why this bauble was so important to you that you risked all to venture into Fortuna."

Holding it up, he angled it back and forth, the stones catching the light and sparking like blue and white fire.

Head slanted, Vanessa cupped his neck.

"Haven't I told you the legend of the sapphire brooch?" She puzzled her forehead. "Are you certain? I thought sure I had."

"No, you haven't." He set the jewel beside the others on her carved rosewood dressing table before nuzzling her neck and then kissing a smoldering path to her bosom. "Tell me now," he insisted throatily in a gravelly timbre that revealed how much he wanted to take her to bed.

Not yet, my fine rogue.

"Stop, knave." Grasping his blond mane, she gave a playful tug. "You know I cannot cobble a single thought together when you kiss me like that."

Heaving an exaggerated sigh, Kingston lifted his head. "Fine, but be swift about it. I have a ravenous hunger that needs satisfying."

He gave her bottom a firm pat.

"*Hmph*. Patience is a virtue, husband."

"The legend, if you please, madam," he purred, beginning to unbutton the impossibly small pearl buttons down the back of her rose-colored gown.

She tossed a saucy glance over her shoulder. "You're living up to your title."

"In what way?" His eyebrows knitted together, a thread of disquiet there.

"Caerleon. Lion. With your blond hair and your tendency to growl or purr."

"Minx," he chuckled, tickling her ribs.

"Stop, Kingston," she giggled. "Or I'll not tell you the legend."

He relented and returned to unbuttoning her gown. "Who is the sot who thought it wise to fasten a gown with so many deuced buttons?"

"It's fashionable," Vanessa said, crossing her arms over her gaping bodice. "Anyway, the legend says that if an unwed man shows the brooch to an unmarried woman and she immediately asks to try it on, she's a foolish choice for a bride. But, if she permits *him* to offer to let her try it on, then she's a wise choice, and he should marry her."

"Wise indeed." A raffish grin accompanied his pronouncement.

She wrinkled her nose. "Although I confess, it's never made much sense to me. The women of my family have possessed the brooch for over a century, and each has worn it on their wedding day."

"Well, mayhap it's time to change the legend then. If a married woman permits her adoring husband to remove the brooch, he's allowed to make love to her."

A satisfied smile quirked his mouth.

"Why am I not surprised that's how *your* legend ends?" Vanessa quipped.

They quite often ended up making love when they'd originally been about another task.

"Finally," Kingston said, unfastening the last of the tiny buttons. "Remind me to forbid you to order any more gowns with more than three buttons."

"Three? You're incorrigible."

"I do my best." He winked, then helped her step from the satin, his blue eyes darkening to indigo in appreciation. "I vow you grow more beautiful every day, love."

Vanessa looped her arms around his neck. "You say that because you love me."

"I say that because it is the truth." He scooped her into his arms and made for their bed. They'd tossed aside convention, scandalizing her servants, and shared a bedchamber.

As it turned out, one of the maids Vanessa had left behind when she'd gone to Canterbury, Marcy Pittock, had been guilty of providing Owen with information and letting him inside the house. The scoundrel had promised to marry the girl, after bedding her, of course. And then once Marcy had begun spying for him, Owen threatened to expose her if she didn't continue to do so.

She'd tearfully confessed all when Vanessa had returned to London in February with her new family, and she and Kingston had interrogated each staff member.

Though sympathetic to the young woman's plight, Vanessa had dismissed her. However, she'd provided a letter of reference and enough funds to see her through until she found another position. Hopefully, she had learned a valuable lesson, for not all employers would've been as benevolent as Vanessa. Marcy Pittock could've found herself in Newgate.

"What are you thinking, darling? You have a faraway look in your eyes." Kingston plucked at the ribbons of her chemise.

"I was thinking of Marcy Pittock and Owen," she answered truthfully. "I still fret that he'll show up and cause problems for us."

"Didn't I tell you not to worry about that blighter?" A scowl pulled his mouth downward, but he brushed his knuckles across her jaw. "But to put your mind at ease, I've had word from the investigator I hired all those months ago. He's traced Owen to New York City."

She glanced up, relief and hope contending for supremacy. Could the only lingering threat to her and Kingston's happiness be truly gone? "In America?"

"One and the same." Kingston nudged her down onto the mattress and set to work on her stockings and slippers, kissing a sensual path down each of her trembling thighs. He was quite the most dutiful and attentive lady's maid.

"Do you think he'll remain there?" she managed to ask before she collapsed back onto the soft mattress.

"I do, indeed," Kingston murmured before kissing

the arch of her left foot. "Seems he owed a great deal of money to some very unsavory fellows here in London. That, combined with your threat to press charges for the theft of your jewels, sent him hightailing it to the States. Where he was apprehended for attempted murder after a petty robbery gone wrong. He's been sentenced to thirty years in prison."

Kingston joined her on the seafoam green and yellow counterpane and, tucking her to his side, draped a long, muscular leg over hers. She adored having his weight atop her.

Despite how awful Owen had always been to her, Vanessa felt a twinge of pity for him.

She rolled onto her side and, wrapping an arm around Kingston's lean waist, gazed into his eyes. "Then, there is absolutely nothing left to keep us from living happy lives now."

"Nothing at all, my love."

Want a FREE first in series Starter Library
from Collette?

Go to: signup.collettecameron.com/TheRegencyRoseGift
to get a five FREE book bundle.

A LADY, A KISS, A CHRISTMAS WISH
Daughters of Desire (Scandalous Ladies), Book One

Sometimes you have to take a few risks on the road to happily ever after…

He dared to defy tradition…

Lord Brandon Morrisette is a born risk-taker. Instead of claiming his place in society, he became a physician to help the less fortunate. So, when he sees a patient mistreating her sweet, bright-eyed companion, Brandon is determined to help bring some holiday cheer into the poor girl's life. It's the least he can do. But in truth, he'd like to do much more for the kind-hearted beauty who so easily captured his attention…and his heart.

She guards a scandalous secret…

Joy Winterborne can't afford to take risks. If anyone found out about her past, she'd lose everything. And getting fired from her companion job would deprive her of the only bright spot in her otherwise dreary life—the time she gets to spend with the charming and oh-so-handsome Dr. Morrisette. Of course, nothing can ever come of her attraction to him. He's nobility, and she's nobody. But that doesn't stop her silly heart from wanting…*more*.

With a little luck, some mistletoe, and maybe even a Christmas wish, can Brandon convince Joy to take the greatest risk of all—falling in love?

About the Author

USA Today Bestselling author COLLETTE CAMERON® is renowned for her Scottish and Regency historical romance novels featuring daring rogues, scoundrels, and the strong heroines who capture their hearts. Her stories are filled with inspiration and humor, making them the perfect escape for fans of Sweet-to-Spicy Timeless Romances®. Living in Oregon, Collette is a confessed Cadbury chocoholic and dreams of spending part of her time in Scotland. From the rugged highlands to the refined drawing rooms of Regency England, Collette's stories transport you to another time and place, where love and adventure are just a page away.

Thank you so much for reading MY DEAREST DUKE. Having lost three family members in house fires, Kingston's grief over the loss of his best friend in a fire was all too real for me. I wanted to create characters in him and Vanessa that you, dear reader, could relate to and come to love as I did.

I mentioned a few characters in the story who have their own books. You'll find Kingston's ancestor, Camden Kennedy's story in my HEART OF A SCOT SERIES. The Earl of Wainthorpe's book is in my FOR THE LOVE OF AN EARL SERIES. The Dukes of Pennington, Bainbridge, Asherford, and Pembroke, and the Duchesses of Kincade and Sheffield also all have books in the SEDUCTIVE SCOUNDRELS SERIES.

I sincerely hope their story brought you a few hours of relaxation and enjoyment. Please consider leaving a review if it did. If you haven't already, I encourage you to read the other books in my Seductive Scoundrels Series.

Hugs,

Collette